Praise for Nthikeng Mohlele's *Small Things*

'Behind this story of love, music and the eternal quest, lies an artistic sensibility as generous as it is complex. The prose is rich in texture, the final effect melancholy and comic in equal proportions.'
J.M. Coetzee

'Nthikeng Mohlele has written a superb second novel in *Small Things*. This book is philosophically interesting, and psychologically astute, demonstrating intelligence and integrity.'
Sarah Frost, *KZN Literary Tourism*

'An unnamed protagonist ... a tragicomic figure worthy of some of the most existentially absurd creations of Albert Camus, Fyodor Dostoyevsky or even Coetzee himself.'
Charles Cilliers, *City Press*

'Lively writing that packs a punch. Mohlele's writing is often superb, crackling with unexpected imagery and a lively inventiveness.'
Margaret von Klemperer, *The Witness*

RUSTY
BELL

Nthikeng Mohlele

UNIVERSITY OF KwaZulu-Natal PRESS

Published in 2014 by University of KwaZulu-Natal Press
Private Bag X01
Scottsville, 3209
Pietermaritzburg
South Africa
Email: books@ukzn.ac.za
Website: www.uknpress.co.za

© 2014 Nthikeng Mohlele

All rights reserved. No part of this publication may be reproduced or transmitted in any form or by any means, electronic or mechanical, including photocopying, recording, or any information storage and retrieval system, without prior permission in writing from University of KwaZulu-Natal Press.

ISBN: 978-1-86914-287-2

Managing editor: Sally Hines
Editor: Sean Fraser
Proofreader: Catherine Rich
Typesetter: Patricia Comrie
Cover design: MDesign

Printed and bound in South Africa by Interpak Books, Pietermaritzburg

CONTENTS

Desirable Horses	1
Sir Marvin at 24	22
Pete Wentzel	34
Consultation Seven	44
Eugene Wentzel	50
Columbus Wentzel	56
Consultation Twelve	73
A Cat Named Clinton K	100
Frank & Maria	114
Sir Marvin at 50	160

For
> My son, Miles Mohlele, who is wise.

DESIRABLE HORSES

I wrestled with life and lost. Not completely, but enough to still have to lie on Dr West's couch every second Friday of the month for the last twenty years. Apart from the occasional long face, in the privacy of my study I am no different from any 48-year-old in any corporate law firm anywhere in the world. I get paid obscene amounts to sniff out loopholes in contracts, litigation minefields that if not detected could obliterate our clients many years in the future. I am a legal soothsayer of sorts, though my formal job description is transaction advice for multinationals. As senior partner, with an ex-officio board seat – for my risk-management skills, I am told – my workload is proportionally related to my six-figure pay cheque, less executive incentives and performance rewards.

My office at Thompson Buthelezi & Brook Inc. is large and tastefully furnished, in oaks and rare artworks. I put in adequate hours, am diligent, keep away from corporate gossip and office entanglements: some of the female colleagues are flirty and beautiful; the CEO, Bernard Parker, tells sexist jokes. My job's all right; I meet interesting people, most of whom say I am one of the best in the business. The work itself is not rocket science, its essence rather straightforward, actually: firmly and officially advise corporates on how to make the most money, without getting burnt. That is not hard. I am busy with a Swedish-Namibian Telecoms merger as we speak: a 60:40 revenue share model. Nothing complicated.

I have a team of young lawyers working for me. I have never met with them, because my instructions are carried out by their bosses, who tell them what to do. Most of their work is good, sometimes average; seldom brilliant. I can tell when my instructions have been diluted, misrepresented – but the slippages are easily fixed: presentation of a Sony cassette to the senior attorney in question, onto which I voice record all my instructions without fail. Located at the heart of the Sandton CBD, TB & Brook Inc. is surrounded by what economists call 'big money' – insurance, banking and mining companies. My office patio overlooks the Johannesburg Stock Exchange, evidence of the ultra rich trapped in a warped bubble.

* * *

My name is Michael. Everyone at the office calls me Sir Marvin. I am the splitting image of my father, who for most of his life had people freezing in their tracks, thinking Marvin Gaye had risen from the dead. Home is in Morningside, eight minutes from work, five if I take the BMW M5. I cannot arrive late at meetings; it is not expected of me to be late – lateness is a disease for other people. I live with Rusty, my lovely wife. Michael Junior, our only son, has recently moved into a penthouse his mother bought him, where I hear they have all-night parties with questionable girls. I let my father speak to him, or my mother, because they understand him better. He has a thing for white girls and chewing gum, something I find rather strange. The chewing gum, I mean.

I have been having a lot of trouble with Michael Junior, although I have to say that some of that abated following his brief incarceration on a drunk-driving charge: shock treatment. I had taken the afternoon off, at Dr West's rooms, when he called, barely audible, the 550i completely written off. That was the firm's BMW and, with insurance not budging, I offered to replace it with an identical car. I drove to the scene, found him reeling with and reeking of alcohol, walking around in his underpants, dictating to paramedics and traffic enforcement officers that he was the son of a respected lawyer, which was true, and that his father would be very upset if they did not let him go, which was false and infuriating.

He could have posted bail the next day, a Thursday, but I insisted that not a soul lift a finger until the following Tuesday, so he had four days to sober up and think about his life. There are times I wish I had such time; the opportunity to completely alter the course my life has taken. 'You let those thugs, those murderers almost kill me!' he yelled at me on his release and, didn't speak to me for eight months – except when he wanted money, of course. Rusty played the diplomat, committed to both sides and yet to neither. I believe he has those parties to spite me, dare me, punish me for things his mother tells him in conspiratorial tones, especially when she is insecure in her diplomatic role, when she is angry with me, when she intentionally serves me burnt toast.

There was a time, years ago, when Rusty loved me. She is, strangely, part of the reason I continue to see Dr West, but not the sole reason by any means. Catherine and Abednego, her parents, are old and sickly – and no longer visit every five minutes. I don't hate them; I just don't like them. Catherine tries, but she is married to a fatally flawed man who is domineering and has opinions on everything – the swine. Three visitor bathrooms, but Abednego will pass them all and stink out my private loo, off my bedroom.

I regularly came home to suffocating smells, until I realised without being told that it was Abednego perching that wobbly rear of his on my loo, door wide open, filling in horse-racing crossword puzzles. I was, in the end, the unreasonable one, unwelcoming, unfriendly.

I pleaded. 'Can't your father use the visitors' bathroom? Please, Rusty.' She sulked, became reckless with the dishes in the sink, and took the M5 keys without asking, leaving me to drive that lumpy piece of metal, her Hummer 3.

I looked like I was driving through a war zone in that thing, tank like, with small side windows, like I was dodging sniper bullets. It was embarrassing parking that monstrosity at important meetings, graced by executive saloons – having to explain my sudden change in vehicular taste. But I digress.

* * *

Dr West probably knows me better than Rusty, the woman who wakes next to me every day. He has aged, has become very candid with me, maybe too blunt. There seems to be no middle ground in how he speaks his mind: promptly, perceptively, passionately. 'You are a respected professional. Desirable Horses will be the end of you. Why can't you rid yourself of these damned whores? Pull yourself together, for God's sake!' He is mean to me sometimes, says I need to understand I am not his only patient, that he does not appreciate being woken at two in the morning because I am having hooker panic attacks. 'Why can't you stop?' he asks me. He has aged considerably, has the impatience of one with no time to waste.

Why can't I? I don't know. I really don't. But I do feel for the poor man. I have put him through a lot: depression of various shades, gloomy suicidal streaks, two alcoholic phases that lasted four and a half years and a peculiar addiction to dangerous behaviour, hazardous activities: 284-kilometre-per-hour blasts along Johannesburg's motorways, eyeballing bouncers who interfered with my lap dances (I am a generous tipper), cooking and devouring mushrooms randomly picked from city parks, and an obscene consumption of filter coffee that resulted in a lingering, natural high.

There were nights I couldn't stand Rusty, when she wouldn't stop complaining that I did not listen to her. Questions: how many stories of rotten teeth and bleeding gums can one listen to over the years and remain intrigued? How many stories of dental reconstructions can one person stand? How many detailed descriptions of mouthwash ingredients, toothbrush design and granny tooth disinfectants can be considered titillating? Of course the ex-Finance Minister is an old client of Rusty's, and of course famous jazz vocalists and newsreaders frequent her rooms; footballers, models, spouses and mistresses, and the general public with tooth preoccupations. Even me. But did I really need to be hearing about it all in minute detail? I told her, years ago, that dentistry was a science limited to teeth, beyond which there isn't much else. Rusty turned the argument on its head. It became a second Vietnam War, a war no one was ever going to win. And there are, to this day, surprise ambushes, unexpected landmines. She and Michael Junior are a two-person platoon; they sulk and reduce everything to one-word answers.

Me: 'Anyone seen my rain suit?' Rusty: 'No.' Me: 'What we gonna do this weekend?' Michael Junior: 'Nothing.' 'Honey, I really feel like being naughty, can we . . . you Sexy Nefertiti you?' Rusty: 'Headache.' Me: 'Hello, Mike. Please give your old man a hand with these groceries?' Michael Junior: 'Television.' I might as well be living alone. I have lost count of how many times I have explained myself to Michael Junior. Explained. Pleaded. Grovelled. To be absolutely honest, I have had very dark thoughts about these two, so dark I have to take midnight showers to rid my soul of impurities.

Just look at this house. Look at it. Isn't it solid evidence of hard work, of a dedicated husband, father? When she is in a good mood, the lovable Rusty, feeling lewd, she stops by at the law firm. I tell secondary lies about a burst geyser, climb into that hideous Hummer and she drives us home. There we follow freshly strewn rose petals in pinks, reds and whites from the front door – a trail of lit candles from the kitchen all the way to our queen-size bed, at the centre of which petals are arranged to resemble a heart. There is even a card, sprinkled with Rusty's rose magic. 'Open it,' she says. The front is a cartoon of an

RUSTY BELL

ice skater, midair. Inside, in brown ink, is written: 'Jump your highest, Sir Marvin. Rusty will always catch you.'

An arrow directs the eye to the very bottom of the card, where it says in small cursive: 'Long fucking completely allowed.' I oblige. We have our shortcuts, you see – because I know every slope, every crevice, every curve of that body – when it is on fire or pretending, when matters become urgent, when to hurry. I am not fooled by the petals: they have nothing to do with romance, and everything to do with coded apologies for the shoddy way I am treated in this house. We crush the petals, claw clothes to the floor. Kiss. Twist and roll. Rusty has never been a complex bed mate, not one with carnal demons intent on all-night toils, but a sensual 38-year-old with the sensuality of a college girl. A few rapid strokes and she loses her bearings, speaks in tongues. She traps me between elegant legs, the colour of mahogany wood under certain light conditions, moans, quivers, surrenders. We stay in bed, like teenagers, and fall asleep in each other's arms. The law firm has the good sense not to call, to disturb me while I attend to plumbing emergencies.

* * *

I meet Abdul Azeez twice a week in my office. He teaches me Arabic. I am, during these sessions, able to travel thousands of years to the Islamic history of Timbuktu. I later ignore Rusty's mood swings and, in the solitude of my study, lose myself in the tales excavated from the sands of the Sahara. Abdul Azeez is an avid scholar and researcher: tall, dreamy, humble to a fault. He has logbooks, bound and precious, detailing important ancient manuscript owners and conservators. Abdul speaks very little, yet when called upon guides me through profound discoveries that often leave me exhilarated. I dabble in ancient philosophy, in law, in poetry. Abdul declines a consultancy fee, yet dedicates four hours every week without fail. The only cost I have incurred for this privilege has been numerous glasses of tap water that Abdul gulps down during our sessions, and a very bad bout of influenza I picked up from him sneezing repeatedly one rainy evening.

I, privately, wish his uncle Aaqil, an old client of ours – oil exploration – was like him; only he is an uptight, impatient, suspicious beast. Grown men run like anxious puppies around him, shielding him with umbrellas, opening the door of his Rolls Royce Phantom, answering his cellphones. That is how I met Abdul Azeez, who had been invited to be his uncle's scribe, because Mr Hakeem does not completely trust lawyers. His reason is direct: hard-earned Saudi money.

Abdul turned out to be a meticulous note taker, quite useful in subsequent Emirates Gas and Niger Oil Consortium meetings, correcting misunderstandings. I warmed to the young man instantly, especially his burgundy ties, Rusty's colour of choice when it comes to brassieres.

* * *

I cannot stand whisky these days. The slightest hint of the smell, the sight of someone clasping a glass, with piss-coloured liquid in ice cubes, makes me ill. My drinking got so bad that my then boss, Mr Chuene, kind but boring, made it his mission to rid me of substance abuse. It was he, upon request of my adorable wife, who suggested that I be checked into a Melville facility — where I wasted valuable time playing chess with lifetime alcoholics. I kept to myself, mostly, but the programme encouraged group things. Diary readings. Hugs. Conversations of various kinds.

I found the clinic's routine torturous, not to mention sitting there on rock-hard wooden chairs describing our feelings to a group of strangers: dissecting, pitying, lying to ourselves. There were moments of brutal honesty, when one grey head with a disarming twinkle in his eyes expressly and responsibly opined that he knew his death would result from drinking, or the after-effects thereof. That his goal was not to stop drinking — because he couldn't, because he had tried all his life, because his father's father died trying — but to drink just enough to reasonably alter sobriety, without being a nuisance. His name was Joseph, or José.

My throat got more knotted with each speaker, for they all seemed to take words out of my mouth. By the time it was my time to speak, to all those slaves of the bottle and addictive powders, words refused to come. The mind was working, the expectation real, from those wounded creatures craning their necks to hear what earth-shattering truths I was about to offer.

But all I could manage was a pained smile, fiddling with the zip of my jacket, staring blankly out the window. With great patience they waited, until I, oppressed by their expectant eyes, finally said: 'I will stop drinking one day. But I, for now, desperately need something to distract me from hanging myself.' There were gasps, some shoe shuffling, then silence. Many hands were extended to me during the coffee break, to which (the coffee) I was also badly addicted, hugs that exposed voluptuous breasts of drinker housewives, a momentary striptease, with which I was also obsessed, and an unrelated conversation about babies, which drove me into a suppressed rage.

* * *

I am a lot more relaxed these days. My Arabic is improving, the household is a lot calmer, and I have beaten all my addictions, but one. I cannot, for the life of me, with all of Dr West's encouragement and rebukes, stop myself from frequenting Desirable Horses. It seems an inbred itch, an insatiable craving, to sit in a dimly lit room, a fine piece of classical music serenading other wretches like me, and succumb to the magnetic pull of beautiful breasts thrust in my face, the mock seduction of those skilled swindlers touching themselves in provocative places, tongues moistening lips, pelvises twitching in choreographed gyrations. I can, between those heavy seconds, totally spellbound, still read the slight frown that momentarily dims the naughty smiles, a frown that gently but firmly says: 'Put more money, you scandalous bastard, this dance is not for free.'

I pull that Simone (not her real name) by the small of her back, closer, so her cleavage stops inches from my nostrils, where sniffing calmly and hungrily, I slip a generous banknote under her brassiere strap. I gesture that she turns around, almost touch her toes, wiggle her perfect bottom in my face, allow me to slide fat rolls of notes, enough for three months' rent in high places, on three sides of her focal points: left and right hips, and of course, just under her navel, where the panty front leads to her forbidden bulge.

Bouncers break necks and arms for errant hands, but I am a law-abiding citizen, so Simone feels safe with me, no matter what the temptations. The bodies are sculptured here, beautiful figures with mesmerising collarbones, steady necks and perfect toes, and navels that look like islands in a calm sea of belly flesh. These girls, Merles, Biancas and Simones, are an addiction I cannot overcome, not even if threatened with impalement.

My introduction into this world, the universe of female bodies, was a rather traumatic affair – one of the reasons, says Dr West, I frequent Desirable Horses: to recapture control, robbed by that sinister encounter. So, I admit I frequent whorehouses, if strip clubs qualify as such, but deny that I have any other intentions other than that addictive, forbidden, magnetic pull. This distinction, contradictory as it might seem, is the sole reason I have Simone's respect, though her frowns are becoming more and more frequent, and her smile too brief these days. So I play by the rules, hand her a note or two. What else can I do?

* * *

When I was younger, twenty or thereabouts, I pictured a very different future to the one I find myself in. It was not a world I imagined would simply fall into my lap. I, until my fingers bled, clawed my way up treacherous mountains of this thing called life. If I had, in that climb for a view from the very top, lost my footing and fallen, there would have never been anyone to avert the calamity. I, as I climbed, knew it would be a treacherous slope, that every step and blind flailing of desperate hands intent on grabbing onto something were all there was to an otherwise unforgiving fall, a fall that would render me deformed and lifeless. I climbed hundreds of precarious rocks, up heart-stopping boulders, unstable and deceptive, only to find thousands of others that seemed to stretch as high as the heavens, as far as eternity.

* * *

My long waltz with whisky has left me with a predisposition to urinary tract infections, something doctors cannot convincingly diagnose or explain. I have spent more time than the average man in front of urinals, something of a mild embarrassment. But there are unexpected distractions. Take this morning. As I stood there, appreciating the slightest spurts, my clammed bladder emptied with delayed pleasure and relief, hosing a lone pubic hair around the urinal, moulding it into impression of letters of the alphabet: a crooked C, an L covered in foam, and as the tool dripped to a halt, something of a confused small letter G. I wondered whose piece of hair that could be. At the same time I was thinking about Rusty.

I think a lot about her these days, that she could in fact be innocent, that it was perhaps too harsh a conclusion to blame her for the depraved, empty and unstable wretch I have become. Yet a crime was committed, a crime she admitted to. I admit, I am damaged. Yet

RUSTY BELL

I can be so very charming. If I didn't say, if you didn't know, you wouldn't suspect that a cynic lurked inside of me. You would be forgiven for thinking I was simply an awkward workaholic, with costly nightlife tendencies.

The trick is simple: I am very charming, likeable in a very understated, pleasant way. It is not an accident that Rusty manufactures stories about burst geysers, that Abdul volunteers keys to the Arabic language, that I have been given the catchy pet name of Sir Marvin, the free lap dances Simone commits to on stage, those prompt hugs from fellow sufferers at Alcoholics Anonymous, the Saudis and the Swedes entrusting me with their billions, and Clementine, my brilliant PA, who swears my Arabic endeavours have steered her thoughts to alternative African history, and Michael Junior, who though a promising composer, is giving serious thought to my request that he not marry young, and to, in case something happens to me, love his mother a little more than is ample – a request I am doing my best to live by.

* * *

It is the second Friday of the month. Dr West and I wasted the first hour of the session disagreeing about the difference between hardened hookers, lap dancers and pole dancers. He, in his religious ways, and with his own selective moral compass, said the very thought of such activities filled him with 'moral apprehensions'. I, on the other hand, told him that I very much wished to be normal, to steer clear of activities so frowned upon, only I was unable to do so because of certain historic mishaps. Though I cannot explain it, or provide details and weighty arguments, I said to him, it felt to me that I needed exposure to the 'apprehensions' for a part of me that was wrecked at the tender age of fourteen. This addiction – an 'annoying delinquency', as Dr West also calls it – is a strange but real need to start again, to, on my own terms, properly introduce myself to women and their bodies – sweet-scented bodies without beer belches, away from the trauma of floor-polish smells.

'But you are going about it the wrong way,' he said today.

I thought, and answered: 'No. Life went around me the wrong way. I am simply effecting corrections. That's all.'

'How are you going to effect corrections to a reputation in tatters?'

'I am 48, Doctor. What if people think me a freak? All I wanted was to find a deeper life. That's all. This very life hung me out to dry. I did not choose any of this. What do you expect me to do? Pretend it didn't happen?'

'No. I expect you to grow up.'

'Easy for you to say. You were not there in that room. You don't know what happened, how dirty I still feel. I am telling you I cannot simply wish this thing away. I am trying – can't you see? I did not choose to be born this way; oversensitive. Life chose that for me. What do you expect me to do? Die? It is an innocent lap dance. That's it. That's where it ends. It's a dance, a 'lewd display', as you say, but a dance nevertheless.

Don't you understand I don't want to be running around this damn country like a horny hound during mating season? I cannot ask my wife to strip dance for me every second day – she's my wife, for God's sake, not a pedlar of 'moral apprehensions'! How the hell d'you think she'll feel, with that kind of disrespect? So it's the strip club. Wrong as it looks and sounds, this is the safer, more responsible option. I took it! Deal with it.'

He jotted a few remarks down, and said: 'Okay, calm down. I hear you. I suggest we continue in our next session. Better if we can do one earlier, to diffuse some of the tension. How goes the Arabic?'

'It goes, interesting discoveries.'

'That's good to hear. Very good indeed.'

* * *

My visits to Desirable Horses are sanctioned by the highest authority: my wife. I took her into my confidence months before pursuance of such liberties. I feel very bad, ashamed, and wish there was another way around my predicament. I could have chosen selected deceptions, misled her without being totally rotten, if such a thing is possible or permissible. She was appalled, outraged and, as she was supposed to be, terribly insulted by the fact that I had, first, the nerve to think about such depraved fantasies, and secondly the temerity to think she would find my indiscretions amusing.

But it was she who on two occasions pleaded that I put the gun down, when I thought I had reached the end of the line. Technically, she is the sole reason I am still alive, the only living soul who understands the gloom that can suddenly befall me, that led to many relapses when I had all but beaten the whisky taunts.

There are times when I cannot understand why she stayed at all, why she punished herself by fighting alongside me, when it was clear the battle was probably already lost. You can understand, therefore, how it feels to let someone of this class down, to propose vile and unsavoury prospects to her. She cried in secret; eyes don't lie.

She was outraged – the tension palpable – then like a judge pondering a life sentence, said: 'I know you have demons, but strip clubs, Michael? What am I supposed to tell your son, if he finds out? What about me? What is my role in this house, in your life, if these are the kind of things you think about? Can't you find something else? Race cars, bungee jumps, learn an instrument; do you have to ogle naked strangers, Michael? I appreciate your honesty. I do. But how do you think I feel? What about *me*?'

I had no answer. I saw the anger build, disbelief mount, and then that hot smack that left my nose bleeding. She started her car and left, switched off her cellphone, disappeared for hours. She returned after midnight, angry but conciliatory: 'Okay, Boo Boo. I don't agree with your mad antics, but you can go. You can go. At least I would know where you are. Don't breathe a word to me about your rendezvous, because if you do that will be your last. Keep it in your pants, your hands to yourself. Be home by no later than 10 p.m. Surrender all your bank cards, except a reasonable cash amount. This cannot go on forever, of course. It has to end in less than a week; I'm serious, failing which no deal. I'm your wife, what do you take me for! Oh, I might also consider an unscheduled inspection, and pray that you observe the spirit and letter of the contract. You're unbelievable. Unbelievable.'

RUSTY BELL

I reached out, kissed her, squeezed those hips of hers, tried to unzip her skirt. A second smack caught me across my right ear, leaving strange whistles blaring: 'Don't do that!' she charged. Some rules will never change: you cannot bed an angry woman. Well, you can, depending on certain variables, but it is bound to be a dreary, solitary affair – mechanical, without grace, devoid of beauty. This is why forgiveness from a woman is such an elaborate affair, cautious and unpredictable – until she feels safe, believes you have paid dearly for your indiscretions.

I never had to endure extended tortures. The reason is simple: I never lied to my Rusty Bell. Not once. I, in at least one other extreme case, got my smacks in advance, did whatever with the purest of conscience. I think I had called her father some unpleasant word; I was promptly smacked, dismissed. Come to think of it, she is not completely innocent, but a brilliant, brilliant tactician – the loveliest of wives. I sometimes think I don't deserve her. I overhear her brag to her friends, when they think I am out of earshot, hear her say: 'My Marvin is a very good man. Wonderful. Trainable.'

* * *

South Africa? Well, things have changed, that's for sure. Even I can see that. It is an increasingly young country, not so chained to its past, a past that like a distant cousin of the holocaust seems like a bad dream from a long time ago. We have a woman president. She has a few character blots here and there, but she's very good. The older generation is dying off, you see – with their knowledge and baggage – making way for an unknown future. But such is life.

My college contemporaries have done very well for themselves; some are in jail, some barely make ends meet. Those were the useless ones, the party animals, who now face the wall, look away or cast their eyes down, whenever I bump into them at the mall. Like I would ask them, 'So, how did you become such a delinquent?'

Some have become lawyers, so a name on some law firm letterhead suddenly rings a bell, and at meetings I meet some, really mediocre yet pompous freaks. But that is no surprise: mediocrity is the new disease in these times. The older folk, busy dying off, prided themselves with vocational matters, with quality and diligence. Not any more. The Michael Junior generation is all about money, money at all costs. There will come a time, I fear, when you cannot trust your lawyer, a surgeon, your financial adviser. Lawyers are supposed to strive to protect and ensure freedom, surgeons to safeguard life itself, advisers to help manage people's money. But the Michael Junior generation seems reckless with these concepts – and not only here, but the world over. What are oaths, standards and rules for if people piss on them?

My son calls himself a composer, yet he cannot play a single piano tune. He feeds numbers into a computer, it spews junk out the other side, and with the help of ecstasy or whatever they sniff or drink these days, sweaty bodies hit the dance floor. The girls don't even bother to wear underwear any more. It's a life without restrictions, freedom without limits. That is why I nearly had a heart attack, when Simone told me she is eighteen. But how, with those full hips, that delightful bust, those eyes and frown that can squeeze money out of a stone? Eighteen? I rest my case.

* * *

RUSTY BELL

Desirable Horses. Quite a name. I understand 'Desirable' – but 'Horses'? Or is it how the club owner sees these young women, as horses, each with a number, running a race? It is clear that a lot of money was invested in the club: its low-hanging floodlights in variations of sensual reds and warm yellows, its comfortable leather couches, the live orchestra that rises from the orchestra pit promptly at 8 p.m., serenading clients with low-key Vivaldi and Mendelssohn favourites. Themed around waterfalls, water tumbles from behind the main stage, where pole dancers perform daring midair splits and somersaults. The club offers head and foot massages on the go, and the dining menu is nothing short of sublime. Simone is in demand, always secured at a hefty premium. That frown of hers, drilling for more banknotes. I am on my hundredth week now, on a first-name basis with girls here. Koreans. Swedes. Mauritanians. Sudanese empresses. South Africans. Brisbane's finest.

I am trying, God knows I am. But I cannot stop. Rusty has gone back to her parents. It has been three weeks now. I am very sad about that. This is why I am drinking again. I was apparently impossible with Mr Hakeem, called him a 'pint-sized Saudi tyrant' – something I don't remember. Mr Hakeem has fired the firm as transaction advisers and, with his back to the wall, Bernard called an emergency staff meeting, and publicly fired me.

I returned home to find a court messenger patiently waiting at the front door. I signed a delivery note, confirming I received the documents. Divorce papers. There was, with the messenger gone, a small envelope on the dining table. I prayed it was not a suicide note; it wasn't. Just my bank cards. Nothing else. I locked the front door, and headed for the shower. I noticed only when it was too late that I was standing under the jets in the shower in my three-piece suit, shoes still on; dripping water, I walked out, collapsed on the bed and wept.

* * *

I woke with a pounding headache, shivering in the still-wet suit. I was about to get ready for work when I remembered that Thompson Buthelezi & Brook Inc. had no use for me any more. I swallowed migraine tablets, showered (again), changed into pyjamas, replaced the wet bedding, and slept for three days straight. I woke on a Sunday afternoon, confused and wobbly. This is the life I lived for 90 days, if not more, until I woke from one of my night binges and found I was still holding a gun against my temple. I had either been too drunk to pull the trigger or lacked the courage to bloody the walls. I smelled eggs, muted kitchen sounds, but dismissed them as hallucinations. With renewed conviction, I held the Beretta 92 – death by Italian pistol design – against my head and begun pumping the trigger. A voice said: 'Breakfast's ready. Come, let's eat and talk, since you're now unemployed.' So my ultimate cure was perhaps written in the stars, preordained.

I had missed Rusty terribly; I tried to kiss her, but she was not amused: 'Stop that!' she warned. Maybe it was Rusty Bell who had been my cure all along. Not Dad. Not Dr West. Not Simone. But again, 48 years is a long time to be alive, two years to half a century. One does not live to be almost five decades without a history of sorts, no matter how bizarre, how incomplete. I wish to, therefore, re-examine The History of Sir Marvin, trace its minutest throbs, its surprisingly desolate landscapes, strewn with carcasses of all kinds.

SIR MARVIN AT 24

Some cravings are, by their nature, reckless: prone to blunders and obscure sorrows, to spine-tingling charms. If you look beyond the surface, pay attention, examine the smallest of details, you would understand an opaque but liberating fact: that nothing can be done about sex, the most unyielding of human hungers.

The campus swarmed with beauties: too varied to allow proper selection, intimate encounters. Of the many fishes in the sea, yet so few, it seemed girls could not be pulled with a net, no matter what waters (dorm parties, cafeterias) burst at the seams, swirling with radiant would-be lovers. They required not a fishing boat, but solitary reflection on river banks: fishing rod in hand, in the company of mosquitoes, boredom and expectation, of patience, waiting for that line to twitch.

Known and generally accepted as a recluse, it was amusing – and, I imagine, shocking – when selected girls learned there were mild perversities perpetuated in their name by my direct questions: 'Tell me something, Rusty Bell, what colour are your nipples?' or the flammable, 'Hello, Monica . . .' then that long oppressive pause, that cool and penetrating gaze, right palm on the heart, as if stopping it from leaping out of the body, then: 'Did you know how painfully beautiful those knees of yours are?'

I got stares. Admonishing. Chuckles. Winks. Embraces. Covert invitations. Gazes of unfiltered admiration. There was some name calling, vehement protests, trivial judgements – at the end of which I calmly and gallantly restated my question or statement, with pleading puppy eyes, to which a Rusty Bell would, charmed, hesitantly respond: 'Honey-brown. Why do you ask?' or a besotted Monica who would, with a beaming smile, say: 'Knees? Oh thank you, Michael, thanks for noticing.'

I would nod, double down in a theatrical bow to Monica, and to Rusty Bell, eagerly awaiting a profound or perverted explanation, and discharge the most speculative of reasons: 'I mentally mistook them to be black, owing to your loveliest of eyes, the tint of precious rubies. I felt obliged to confirm, and in so doing lay to rest mischievous thoughts that could arise, if such curiosities are left unchecked, to bloom. In brief then, it is out of duty and my loathing for the secret perversions some men inflict on honey-brown-nippled treasures of your ilk, Ms Bell.'

'Maybe you should kiss me sometime,' she said, her head slightly tilted.

'Tempting,' said I. 'But I don't do rushed kisses. I much prefer kisses slow, so they linger for at least three years after the fact.'

'Explain,' she said, frowning.

I told her that my real area of interest was first and foremost perfectly architectured collarbones. That there was nothing more beautiful than feminine collarbones that complement a longish neck, even more so if such a neck is adorned with pearls. Skilled fashionistas run one or two circles of the pearl gem around the neck, ending the tapestry with a knot, a constellation of pearls that rests halfway down the chest, in the middle somewhere, before the mammary estates begin. Beautiful collarbones, I continued, perfectly aligned to contours of the jaw line and the bottom tips of ears, are the most erotic of things – not like breasts, things grabbed by lesser mortals at the slightest hint of desire, without the faintest thought. Collarbones, on the other hand, are delicate and neutral places of worship, subtle yet potentially explosive, if nibbled with the right measure of teasing. Rampant skirt chasers would not know this, I assured her, for the skill rested on inquisitorial preoccupations: what are the effects of kisses on collarbones? Which are the routes a kiss should travel, even with a predetermined destination to the lips? Surely the ear lobes are worth a nibble or two? And what are jaw lines for if not boulevards to flow kisses onto twitchy, magnetic lips? Now the answers: with great patience and true mastery, a kiss should begin at the shoulder blades, work its way over the shoulders, the ears, the jaw lines (yes, both), a dip under the chin, a sprint to between the eyes, another drop to the left collarbone, then the right, a U-turn to the left cheek, before a cautious and intense approach to a quivering and parted mouth, just as skilled pilots direct giant aircraft onto runways.

Rusty's heart galloped away, and trying to rein it back, she confessed: 'Never before has a potential insult sounded so sweet. I am torn between scratching your eyes out or letting you see things few mortals are privileged to touch, let alone lick. You have talent, I give you that, but be sure to use it wisely. But, again, lust can turn the most timid of men to passionate poets,' she said blushing. 'Feminine hearts can be unmovable boulders. Or shaky, unpredictable, starved things.' She winked, and was gone.

* * *

I had, that summer, almost perfected selected contemplations that, by chance, rattled the hearts of girls. The glow, the very premise of my ponderings at times included historical events, dictators of every kind, dirty old men, determined skirt chasers. A certain purity, a sacredness of sorts, does not allow me extended explanatory liberties, which is not to say observance of such limitations has a bearing on my rather colourful life lessons, false discoveries, even occasional calamities of the carnal kind.

* * *

Seen from apartment blocks and other high-rise buildings, suburban Johannesburg is, in part, an expansive canvas of mansions on sloping hills, prostituting itself to an abundance of trees. The view is flattened by city lights come night, dissolving the landscape and architectural details into a fuzzy, yet picture-perfect glittering so pretty it deceives the eye into seeing beauty. Once in a blue moon power outages expose the picturesque illusion for what it is: a paradise indebted to light bulbs. Darkness shatters the myth, exposes the city's nocturnal ambience to be a fraud, the spellbinding lights an unreliable measure of civilisation. The city collects rates from residents — to revive worn wiring and substations roasted by lightning and decades of service, for control over neon lights so hopelessly dependent on substations surviving lightning strikes.

It rained: thunderous storms that shot travelling lightning nerves over the cityscape, lightning dipping fiery fingers onto tree tops and into swimming pools, lazy and laborious drizzles favoured by couch potatoes, windy hail storms that gave insurance companies heart tremors, downpours that threatened to wash bridges and rose bushes away. It rained because it needed to rain, because rain inspired poets and blooming trees, drizzled because that is what rain is supposed to do: rain. I should have slept; rebelled, pretended I was not awaited at the rooms of Dr West: that condescending, judgemental, brilliant bastard.

* * *

Consultation 34. Dr West telephoned Dr Moroka and put him on speaker. They exchanged cordialities, generalities: that Obama was in trouble with the US economy, that Philip Roth had retired, clinical trials on some drug meant to counter Parkinson's. Dr Moroka said there was a bridal shower for his sister Beulah, to which Dr West was invited. Those two: who would have thought they knew each other, related after office hours, exchanged stories about the world's sick and troubled? The small talk out of the way, commentary on things they had no control over, Dr West intimated that I was by his side, listening in, to which Dr Moroka said: 'Hello, Michael, I pray you have been eating.'

RUSTY BELL

I mumbled something, before Dr West prompted him to share his latest observations. Dr Moroka drew deep breath, and burdened, spoke directly to Dr West, but on occasion, switched to 'Michael and I talked at length about this', which I believe was meant to make me feel part of the proceedings. Dr Moroka spoke of a chemical imbalance triggered by too little food, bowel disorders, 'a concerning and potentially damaging loss of weight'. The worst, said Dr Moroka, '. . . is unknown dangers and future complications that might arise out of depriving the body of critical nutrition'. He concluded that he was gravely concerned; 'exasperated' was his exact word, 'that such a fine and obviously bright young man should place himself against the tide of normal living'. Quite a linguist, that Dr Moroka.

It was his recommendation, therefore, that Dr West continue engaging me in an effort to uproot underlying causes, because 'problems with diet and insomnia were symptomatic of a much deeper problem'. The predicament was, according to him, primarily psychological. It was at this point that I ventured an opinion: 'Good morning. Allow me to interject, Dr Moroka. Obama is not in trouble with the economy. The economy is in trouble with itself, with capitalism. His job is unfortunate, as was Clinton's, Reagan's, Mbeki's — and all the others before and yet to come. About Roth: writers never retire; they just stop writing, but continue reflecting, ruminating, offering insight into obscure social irritants. That is the lifeblood of art. It does not begin or end with a pen. I know little about Parkinson's, except that all disease makes a mockery of life and fairness in the allocation of such burdens to some and not to others.'

That said, I coughed, a shallow wet cough, and told them, in a tone free from grandeur, lacking in pastoral pulpit pretensions, that I understood and empathised with their dilemma. That they should not feel obliged or bound by medical ethics and oaths, for we were all – them included – merely dust in waiting. That when we had perished, our knowledge of American state affairs notwithstanding, we were but food for worms, bones that would become one with dust. That didn't, however, mean that we should be reckless in our existence, or cause anxiety – no matter how peripheral – to those willing and elected to be guardians of normal living. Doctors, for instance.

They were right to be concerned, a fact I revered, yet in safeguarding me and their trade, they had forgotten to consider, to be daring, to ask, if food was all there is to existence. That formula is wrong, or at least incomplete, I told them. Haven't they wondered why, after many years of mounting their wives, their secret muses, their lust refused to gather cobwebs? Does the breast, knowing in the language of caress, of wondering salacious tongues of men, know brown sugar and what it is for? Dr West put his notebook down, took off his glasses, rubbed his eyes intensely, leaving his knuckles whitened and his brow reddened. Dr Moroka managed a low-key 'My dear God in heaven!'

'If,' I continued, 'humanity, or more specifically men and women in white coats, in laboratories, continue murdering mice, infecting them with all sorts of plagues, why are we so appalled if all I am doing, or trying to do, is to sacrifice me and me alone, and hopefully benefit the seven billion souls and counting, who would never know how it feels like to be a mouse swimming in bacteria? Only the "bacteria", in our case, or what Dr Moroka refers to as the tide of normal living, is the fact that the search for the fullness of existence does not have a name. It is not a medical science. But believe me when I say, and I know I don't have conclusive proof, that what we call our lives, our health, our being, are but fragments of so great a mystery as dry oceans. So we have invented pills for all sorts of banalities (to force sleep, prevent births, to clear pimples): but what does that tell us about life? Very little, I suggest. That means there is and has to be another way, a yet-to-be discovered path, a beam of light that will once and for all answer: what is life hiding from us? Why does the breast know particular kinds of touches and explorations, and not others: like the coarseness and sweetness of sugar granules, for instance? Dr Moroka was at great pains to suggest that I must not confuse hallucinations from hunger, tricks a starved mind play on its owner, with insight of a higher existence. Maybe you are right, Dr Moroka. But what if you are wrong? Let's think about that. We might just discover, while we are at it, a new frontier to life. That's all.'

Both doctors sighed. Dr West fidgeted. And that is where it should have ended. But Dr West excused himself, forgetting his mobile phone on the coffee table, for a trip to the urinals. My fingers itched . . . Who do psychologists have as friends, who do they talk to? I glanced around, invaded the iPhone. I knew the quickest way to establish the most important people to Dr West, and checked all names under speed dial, which were at first unremarkable: Bridgett Chaplain, Detective Jones, Sandton Pharmacy, Jennifer Piano Instructor, Mowbray Police Station, Mommy, Bedrock Capital . . . and things got a bit more interesting with: Sexy Betsy, Grill Restaurant Lucy, and Airport Prune-

Boobed Isabella. I was on Pastor Abrahams, past Jude Plumber 2, my thumb furiously flicking towards Midnight Dulcinea and Bad Debt Plague, when I heard Dr West's footsteps. I placed the phone on the glass coffee table, feigned boredom.

Dr West looked at me in a new light. I was not sure if his hesitant scrutiny of me had to do with the phone, or my heartfelt lecture about breasts and brown sugar. He said he was starving, suggested I join him for early lunch at The Grill House downstairs. We shuffled among Sandton City crowds, between sinfully wealthy shoppers purchasing porcelain figurines, past pretenders sinking deeper into credit card debt. Everything around me, before me, above me, seemed out of focus, a misty blur, as we walked past toddlers pushed around in expensive prams, past romance exhibitionists frolicking down escalators, bored shop-front promoters of perfume and cutlery brands, the odd policeman chewing gum. Past luggage shops our journey proceeded, past candy outlets, the banking court, and down a lift whose doors open onto The Grill House entrance, largely deserted, except for a reserved birthday lunch table.

Waitress Cordelia, a bubbly young thing with dimples and a bouncy walk, led us to a secluded corner table, opposite which a giant windmill painting hung. Dr West ordered lamb shank, with couscous and some stir fried vegetables. He gently pushed my menu to me. Aromas, no doubt catchy, wisped from the kitchen, drowning me in an avalanche of nausea. I avoided my reflection in the mirrors, since I knew what I looked like; saw no need to keep checking.

'Just water and lemon for me,' I told Cordelia.

'No!' countered Dr West emphatically, half authoritative and a touch careful. 'Please, Michael, a small meal won't hurt. This is supposed to be your treat. What do you say?' I shook my head, and when Cordelia returned she placed a glass in front of me, water with ice and sliced lemons. Four rapid gulps later, I felt commotion in my depths, bowels shrugging off the water, resulting in ocean-like upheavals, swirling foams, ending in eminent vomit. I excused myself, wobbled latrine ward. My body rattled, somehow dissolved into itself, like an erosion of the bones, making my step unsteady, my vision blurry. I had barely reached the pot, sprinting past a Martin Amis look-alike, before emptying the lemon water and the previous evening's canned peaches, in four forceful bellows. The world rotated beneath my feet, tilted at oblique angles, leaving distant rumbles in my head. Mr Amis fixed a tie in front of the communal mirror, the greasy taps servicing all manner of hands, hands with their assortment of impurities: tours down defecation avenues, unknown horrors from clammy and sweaty handshakes with strangers, remnants of dandruff under fingernails, precarious scratches of groins.

'Dude, you okay?' ventured Martin Amis.

I gazed at him, his office demeanour, and answered: 'Why?'

'Pardon me, but you look like you've walked to Mars and back!'

'Maybe I have, or just might consider it,' I said.

'Shit, man, whatever it is, please take care.'

I chuckled, felt mocked, said: 'Oh well, nice of you, I didn't get your name . . .'

'Amos. Amos Levine. J.P. Morgan, Africa Division.'

'Thanks, Amos. I'm fine.' He half waved, and was gone.

Back at the table Dr West nibbled on a grilled calamari starter. I had barely taken my seat when he announced that Rusty Bell had, in confidence, given him a copy of my last email. He said he had read it, 26 times, and yet found he couldn't quite wrap his head around its true purpose, its unusual tone. The story about the leaf, he continued, a piece of calamari impaled on a fork midair, is like nothing he had ever encountered, not in literature or in conversations. That close, obsessive observation of the leaf, its pores, its veins, suggested to him that I was not a normal patient, that behind my surface eccentricities there seemed, to his mind, something puzzling, though he couldn't put his finger on it. I would make a great writer, he opined, and added – the fork parking the calamari piece in his ravenous mouth, followed by two quick wipes with the napkin, a thoughtful sip of wine – that he was worried, feeling helpless, that such insight, whatever its imperfections, would go to waste.

Feelings of great intensity can coexist with a more balanced, gentler view of life. Speaking as a friend and he supposed a father figure of sorts, as a fellow human being, not as a head doctor, he didn't think it was wise to drain life of all its inherent pleasures, to peel the bark from which it covers itself, exposing things without form or meaning. He thought Rusty Bell was lovely, concerned – as he was – about someone she cared about deeply. He would understand if I was mad at Rusty Bell for leaking my deepest thoughts, but if it made any difference, he would have acted in the exact manner to come to a friend's aid. He hoped it was not too late for me to adjust my views, that I was not too close to the brink. What did I think about that? Well, said I, my fasting was never intended to be an open-ended crusade, it always had limits. It was pointless to suffer for things one would not be around to witness, though history disproved that conclusion on many levels, across continents. There was always, pun intended, a leaf to be taken from solitary, insignificant mad men. With due respect, I told Dr West, he had done well in treating me, but that it was, however, my considered opinion that he had misdiagnosed me: also totally missed an opportunity to rethink medical science. There was nothing new in the shock and trauma resulting from Pete Wentzel resorting to such a heavy-handed solution to his earthly misgivings. I don't know anything about psychology, I told him, but I held a view that all of medical science was not life, but an effort to enforce balance when nature imposed chaos. That was – beside the fact that I wished to discontinue therapy, return to normal life, to eating – all I wanted to say.

Dr West's eyes watered. I could not tell if it was emotion (which?) or fatigue. I apologised for what would have seemed like bad manners, excused myself and stood up to leave. Dr West raised an open palm, said wearily and reflective, 'I hear you, Michael. Please sit. Psychology has been around for a very long time. It's not something you change willy-nilly because one patient has personal passions. It is quite different to discarding chewing gum. In many ways, our very existence depends on it. On sane people. But, again, what if we are indeed wrong? Or worse – and not that I am referring to you – but how dangerous is it to listen to people who might not necessarily be in the best frame of mind, resulting in catastrophic mistakes? Think about it.'

'Yes,' said I, 'psychology has been around for a very long time. But so has ignorance.' I shook his hand and left.

PETE WENTZEL

It was heart-wrenching visiting Pete, Columbus' father. We sat in silence, on reed chairs on the veranda of his Auckland Park home. He offered a tour of the house, said: 'You don't know a man unless you have dined in his home.' He showed me a handful of Columbus' childhood pictures in which Columbus looked suspiciously at the camera, his curls framing a chubby but wise face. His room was sparsely furnished: A bed. An antique reading table. A tennis racquet on the cream wall. Angus Young, the goldfish, glided in a modest aquarium. A wire dustbin with curls of orange peel. On the reading table was an out-of-focus picture of Kate, Columbus' mother, sprawled by the poolside, cigarette in hand, next to a Blaupunkt stereo, from the depths of which Dylan strummed his guitar, made love to his harmonica. There wasn't much else. Yet the Columbus persona loomed large. There seemed to be a profound aura, a knowing calm about the room, knowing in that Columbus knew so much, yet said so little. It was a room, as rooms are rooms, partitioned portions of houses, to foster privacy, to safeguard pleasures and personal idiosyncrasies, detachments from shared family rituals. Dinners. Prayers. Futile mealtime debates: against the perils of taxation. It was a room in a house built with Pete's schoolmaster's wages, furnished with Kate's chef earnings. It was a room in an average suburb, buzzing with second-, third- and fourth-hand cars, a neighbourhood with forlorn dogs, a place of over-indebted, insomnia-ridden cynics with peptic ulcers.

But Auckland Park was nothing compared to the Alexandra of my childhood. In pursuit of meaning, purpose, there were many Nelson Mandela and Churchill namesakes in torn jerseys with watery noses running the streets of Alexandra. These Mandelas, with ashy twig limbs and yellowing teeth, with unkempt nails and ringworm, with bloodshot eyes and mute tendencies, were what life really looked and smelled like when stripped of all its perfumes and gluttonous dinners. Things had gone beyond survival in parts of Alexandra, where life galloped away, regardless of the Churchills surviving months without as much as a bar of soap. What becomes of such people, Churchills who once passed time by drawing fire engines and food impressions in the dirt? Columbus' Auckland Park was also tragic, in moderation: the rusty gates, the neglected lawns, sheriff ultimatums in letter boxes. This was a world Columbus called home, the same world Kate escaped in pursuit of Houghton snobbery – Houghton with its automated garden sprinklers and grand mansions, its driveways adorned with Bentleys and Audis, a world of esteemed and eminent persons. Judges. Bankers. CEOs of corporations. Houghton residents were too busy to think beyond the next day, to – like Columbus – reflect on death and burials, how to dismantle known and accepted truths. Such ponderings were choked by obscene displays of wealth and corporate slavery. Eighteen-hour work days. High blood pressures. Fragile marriages. Overweight offspring. Overstocked wine cellars. Expensive divorces. By-invitation-only house-warming parties: to parade new lovers and imported cigars. The odd assassination. High stakes.

This I saw during our visit to Kate, the day I witnessed Columbus wounded by his mother's disloyalty. We debated whether Kate ever loved Pete, and concluded that it was possible that she did, but that she reserved greater love for money and Dr Coetzee, a man whose life mission was to stop drooping breasts and buttocks, drain human fat from well-fed housewives, target eye bags, stretch unwanted lines to enforce youthful looks, declare war on facial moles and imperfect noses, attack facial hair with laser beams, chop ballooning bellies. Dr Coetzee also had a network of fellow doctors and specialists qualified in correcting the omissions and excesses of nature. Dentists. Nutritionists. Dermatologists. Psychiatrists. Kate looked very happy in her new palace on Money Boulevard. It was not hard to see that she gave no thought to Pete and his 1970s' Datsun. She had eyed Dr Coetzee's millions under the guise of D-cup transplants, while Dr Coetzee saw a cougar with legs that warranted ferocious nibbling, fondling. Pete lost. Columbus was wounded. Father and son, at different times, confided in me with similar resignations: people are unknowable. Little did Kate know that she would perish from massive internal bleeding, following botched tummy-tuck surgery. Her passing charred Pete, who had still not recovered from her walking out of a sixteen-year marriage. Columbus' passing, barely six months later, was too much for Pete to bear.

RUSTY BELL

I observed Pete as we sat on the veranda of 103 Avalanche Drive, chewed by loneliness and grief. He never said a word about Kate, and only a few about Columbus. There seemed to be permanent tears in his eyes, as he brought tea and biscuits, did his utmost to be a good host. Yet family pictures attested to happier times: Kate smiling in Pete's firm embrace during some game drive, Columbus chasing Pete with a hosepipe, evidence of hysterical laughter at Columbus in Elvis Presley attire during a birthday karaoke session. I know it meant something to Pete that I shared my Columbus moments with him; though I never knew for sure what level of solace Pete felt I availed.

He had questions: what did the lecturers think of Christopher's IQ? Because he was so private, how was he with and around girls? What did he believe was his greater purpose in life? Girls adored Christopher, I told him, though Columbus remained ambivalent in matters of love and courtship. It was as if he knew he had limited time. IQ? Columbus had a mind that reasoned beyond known possibilities. The lecturers loved this, of course; they encouraged him, learned from him. The answer to Columbus' greater purpose in life remained elusive, suffice to say that he believed in happiness. That drew a lone tear from Pete, before he said, 'Giving. My boy was a giver, not a taker. My boy gave, by the bucketful. I am not sure this world deserved him, if it repaid him for being such a fine soul.' Most of the time, Pete wrestled his grief, and there were occasions when not even the sweetest details about Columbus' life reached him. He sat on that veranda. Unshaven. Perspiring. Sorrowful. Like he had swallowed rust. Events at Chris Hani High, where he was headmaster, added to his misery. Not only did he have to deal with a disloyal dead ex-wife and son, but had to stomach shepherding uninspired teachers, cautioning learners that were increasingly living on the edge, calming enraged parents who suddenly discovered their sweet little angels were whoring drug peddlers.

It was his problem if the plumbing was blocked, his problem if teachers suffered marital fallouts, his problem if some school bully overplayed their hand, his problem if some kids were dull and stupid. It was his headache if the same raging parents left loaded guns within reach, his nightmare if bullies experimented with the real effects of gunshot wounds. No one praised him when Chris Hani High earned splendid grades, yet most blamed him when thunderstorms gutted school property: 'When last did he bother to check the school's insurance policy?' they charged. Didn't he know that life was synonymous with acts of God? How could they be sure that he cared for their children, if the school was under-insured? They complained about overcrowding and, through the PTA, mandated him to review exorbitant insurance premiums in favour of more classrooms, and when the storm hit turned around and accused him of reckless investment. Some sued him. Some wagged fingers in his face. Some sent hate mail. Some demanded written public apologies. Others stood firm, defended his blotless, selfless commitment to Chris Hani High.

Kate slow roasted him with her very public affair, her unmistakable affections for Dr Coetzee. Bankrupted by legal fees (sued twice), the sheriff and a multitude of collections agencies also began leaving embarrassing 'Final Notice' letters with blood-red stamps on his gate. Debt counselling followed shortly after, followed by Kate moving out. It had been a dark time in Columbus' life, too. The

History of Art class mistook his silence for drug-induced brooding – only to discover, months after his funeral, what the silence was truly about.

Pete, in not so many words, begged that I sleep over, share a meal with him. It was an odd request, somewhat out of place, yet not entirely unimaginable. It was obvious his very marrow throbbed with loneliness and surrender: how his garden was choking with weeds, how the veranda was invaded by leaves, how he paid no heed to a letter box jammed with mail, how his newspaper subscriptions lay yellowing on the overgrown lawn, how the dustbin in Columbus' room still held blackening orange peels from months ago, how he turned a blind eye to teachers slacking off.

His grief was engraved on old and neglected potatoes growing green offshoots in the pantry, palpable in his unpolished shoes, hovering in the swimming pool green with algae, in the broken kitchen windowpane that invited rain and dust into the house, in the hollowness of his many Best Headmaster Awards. Our meal, roasted Woolworths chicken, rye bread and wine, was a rare glimpse into Pete's desperation, how he was increasingly drowning in insomnia, crawling through life with a mouth full of clenched teeth.

It was over the rye bread dinner that Pete, his tongue loosened by red wine, divulged that there was a visitor in his bedroom. Mmabatho, a Geography teacher he had admired, hired and fired, now visited him once a week, for company and advice at first, followed by fond sitcom rituals, the vivid possibility and necessity of therapeutic sex, the pursuit of which always ended in self-conscious fondling and shallow excuses: the pillows being too hard; the fluorescent bulbs flickered a little, thus disrupting sustained lust; or Mmabatho's nine-year-old knee surgery, from which she had made a full recovery.

Mmabatho was, according to Pete, 43, full-figured, with smallish brown eyes, youthful facial features. She also taught Life Skills to Grade Nines, the first black teacher on his staff compliment post-1994. Pete skirted details of why he had fired Mmabatho – except to say 'unfortunate and inappropriate things happened'. He quickly changed the topic, asked more Columbus questions: what was closest to Christopher's heart, if he intended on getting married, his views and sensibilities about children. About politics. The more Pete probed, the more he dug, for the fading glitter of his deceased son, the more the grief froze his Adam's apple, the more he swallowed words, courted obvious lapses in composure.

Were his questions, his gentle yet relentless interrogations, testimony to Columbus having been too private a child, pleasant, yet unknowable? Why did he not simply ask him: Son, what is the closest thing to your heart? What good were my second-hand answers to Pete? Was I at liberty to ask him what Mmabatho was doing, hibernating in his bed? What exactly were the 'unfortunate and inappropriate things' that warranted dismissal yet encouraged siestas in his bed? Columbus and I never discussed children or politics, I told him. No matrimonial debates, either. I felt burdened, by this resurrecting Columbus business.

'It is just that things have changed,' he said in mild drunkenness. 'This has become a very admirable but brutal country. The politics matter: who you marry matters, because it is ultimately about children who will be born in 2088. Our lives are their inheritance. How certain are we that the South Africa of 2088 will survive our current malaise: nine-year-olds giggling at obscene video clips on cellphones, cocaine addicts masquerading as meek loners, Grade Eights flirting with amused teachers? That was unheard of in our times! Teachers were beacons of enlightenment, bastions of authority! Not any more. Which is horrifying, because most life lessons are learned at school. You think these things are simply misguided urges, until teachers start getting crumpled notes, crude overtures.

'And the parents? It's always the school's fault, me being asleep on the job. Why are children allowed to sniff their teachers' bottoms as they correct mathematical mishaps from dull and uninspired would-be dropouts? It's as if they're born knowing, their lives acts of *being* and not of *becoming*. Perils of the information age, a world without secrets. Yet the parents refuse to acknowledge this – still expect that schools are bubbles of innocence. But bubbles burst. I have seen many bursts. Stabbings. Abortions. Emotional meltdowns. Even rapes.'

Pete bid me a good night at 11.45 p.m., stood to attend to his mysterious visitor, a visitor sidelined from our dinner. I took a leaf from Pete's suffering: why do people, whole societies, look suspiciously at unmarried people if getting married implied untold dilemmas? I, on closer inspection, after days of fasting and lucid reflection, also concluded that there was, in fact, little whoring taking place on campus. That such acts pointed not to a second sexual revolution, greater in proportion and daring to that which, in the sixties, erupted from the pill and rock 'n' roll. What seemed from a distance like rampant fornication were, in fact, voyages of self-discovery, expressed with youthful arrogance and daring, crude enough to be mistaken for something far more sinister. What did young adults know about sex and its place in the greater scheme of existence? Did their pursuit of newly discovered sensations, their God-given right to pleasure, so blind them that they only managed elementary secrets of the carnal universe, a universe fraught with thrills and condemnations as to wreck whole lifetimes? The attainment, the temporary possession of sensual powers, fooled both participants and onlookers that the campus was under siege – polluted by ambitionless imbeciles more concerned with campus porn (*Return of the Fucker Boys* seemed a favourite) than learning important world treaties.

Did they not know, I debated with myself, that there were far greater and profounder reasons for living? I reflected: was Pete's despair, his eminent collapse, his helpless rage, what is meant by life in the Real World? Was growing old a sadistic noose that choked life out of the Pete Wentzels of this world, a millionth of a breath at a time? That, amid breathtaking beauty, moments of tenderness and discoveries, existence was also about fate, of which there is absolutely no control? Was it Pete's fate to, at 73, suddenly discover a class with African children alongside the Krugers and Cloetes, to in his twilight years be held responsible for triumphs and tragedies affecting the Smiths, Mositos and Kubekas? Was it his fate to speak through translators to overjoyed or weeping next-of-kins; for cultural shocks that awaited him at Indian funerals and celebrations?

He, Pete, was like a giant shock absorber, soaking the minutest Chris Hani High tremors, echoing in his own Real World. His neck was always under the guillotine. Learner fights. Health scares. Toxic teacher love affairs. Even acts of God. Sleep came easy for me in

Columbus' old room. I thought I was dreaming, but wasn't. I heard it. Every bump against walls, the furniture, the almost muted shrieks of gleeful gasps. Sixto Rodriguez drowned most of the details, but some sounds are primal, instinctive, unmistakable. Pete groaned like a wounded beast, mounted Mmabatho like his existence depended on it, the brutal routine momentarily lapsing into low-key murmurs, before erupting into extended, ferocious, erotic acrobatics. I feigned coughing, clearing my throat. Finally! I thought. Something to ease Pete's misery, to rid him of his lethargic decay.

The blinking, blood-red numbers on Columbus' digital clock said 3.08 a.m. I was once again seized by towering sleep, sleep that reduced me to a log. I was awoken by a loud explosion. My bewilderment was rocked by yet another explosion, followed by Mmabatho's uncontrolled hysteria. I ran to Pete's room, dazed and naked, kicked the locked door open, and right there, my misery began.

CONSULTATION SEVEN

I should have slept, rebelled, pretended I was not awaited at Dr West's rooms, Room 143B, Sandton Medical Towers, 11.30 a.m., eight weeks after the explosions. A small wooden speaker whispered orchestral music, barely audible. I lay on the couch, completely numbed. Audrey, Dr West's receptionist, offered me filter coffee, which only worsened the situation, the caffeine setting my nerves ajangle. Audrey indicated Dr West would see me in a moment. He soon entered, glancing at his wristwatch, notepad in hand, smiling as he settled on a rocking chair opposite me.

Glass-walled consultation rooms. Portraits of influential persons on the walls. Juvenile tree-fern pot plants. Silver-lettered bluish medical journals, filing cabinets brimming with patient files: all manner of anxieties and disorders. I could smell a trace of incense. On the walls were degrees earned from notable universities: Cape Town. Oxford. Melbourne. Harvard. It was evident that Dr West was handsome in his youth, a privilege that has only matured with age: tall, slim built, in expensive suits and fruity cologne, a wealth of greying hair, and spotless fingers that occasionally dragged the Parker across the pages of the leather-padded notebook, that once in a while adjusted his rimless John Lennon spectacles with small, gentle, unobtrusive movements.

'Let's go back a bit. You heard the gunshots, the lady screaming, ran to Pete's room, and . . . ?' I shivered: 'I saw blood, a little pinked out, like strawberry yoghurt on the walls. I only realised moments later that I was looking at brain matter, too.' Dr West did not wince one bit: 'Go on . . . Describe the scene as you remember it. No pressure and, you can stop anytime if you need to.' I sipped coffee.

'I was shocked. Scared. Traumatised. I had heard them being intimate at around 3 a.m., but nothing seemed . . . well . . . obvious, that something was wrong. I mean, I didn't know Mr Wentzel that well; I was friends with his son. Dogs were barking. I triggered an alarm en route to his room. It was all confusing and bewildering. Mmabatho was huddled in a corner, hiding behind a laundry basket, also in the nude. There was a spilled wine bottle on the floor, Mmabatho's sandals. I ran to the kitchen and rang the police – but wasn't sure if it was a murder or suicide. I learned everything else from newspaper reports, from Mmabatho's statements to the police. That it was both attempted murder and a suicide. Mmabatho was herself fast asleep at the time. One bullet wound to the stomach, the fatal one through the temple. 3.6 Magnum. An officer on the scene said: "It blasts a crater into its victim's head." He was right. A whole portion of Pete's head was blown off. Like Kennedy. I was then taken to the hospital by paramedics on the scene and treated for shock. That's when Dr Moroka gave me your card, said he recommended I come and see you.'

'How are the nightmares, since you began taking the anxiety and sleeping tablets?'

'Better. But I'm dizzy most of the time.'
'Are you eating properly?'
'No.'
'What would you say is your level of nervousness, on a scale of one to ten?'
'Nine and a half.'
'After the medication?'
'Maybe seven.'
'You dream about Columbus?'
'Sometimes.'
'What dreams?'
'Walks. Talks. Lecture-hall scenes.'
'And your disagreements with Rusty?'
'Catastrophic.'
'Why do you think Rusty and you fight, or rather disagree so much?'
'I don't know.'
'Are you intimate with her, in the physical sense?'
'No.'
'What does such intimacy mean to you, personally?'
'It is relentless fumbling in pursuit of erotic electrocutions, meant to imprison and magnify pleasure. It seldom does, though, this search for carnal sanctuaries. Men allow gross violations of their lives. All the pleading, the bribery, the gifts – all the cajoling and inward rage of wanting, beseeching and thirsting to be between the legs of women is depressing.' The Parker pen recorded salient points.

'A heartfelt definition,' said Dr West. 'But what if I told you, not my words but words of a Yemeni poet, not famous, Yael something, who says that sex is the closest thing to eternity, a vibrant tapestry of the rarest sensations that torches the soul in abundant ways, giving that freeing, fruity, fuzzy feeling?'

I did not answer, except to say that I didn't know anything about Yemeni poets and fruity, fuzzy feelings. The session ended with Audrey bringing some bottled water and dried fruit, while Dr West scribbled notable observations in his calm, reflective manner. Amazing how he asked seemingly unrelated questions, only to join the dots three sessions later, with devastating clarity and detail; strange how we kept going back and forth on things, what I thought to be negligible details.

There was one observation I kept from Dr West, a detail I found particularly interesting. I had noticed, in passing, amid the police sirens and alarm pandemonium, that Pete had discarded the see-through glass plate and tall wine glass, from which I had the Woolworths chicken and red wine just hours earlier, into the garbage bin. Would he, when he had sucked her dry, have discarded Mmabatho, too?

* * *

Not a single day passed when I did not think of Columbus. It was not grief, but a sense of mild depression; a sudden loss of interest in campus thrills known and confirmed to engender purpose in boys. Even Rusty Bell was spared my word tap, which dripped to a halt, leaving an echoing silence. There were times when I held her tight, so tight that I feared I would crush her, but then there were moments when I wanted nothing but absolute silence, solitude. I sealed my ears with cotton wool, blocked off unwanted sounds. I left the world, one sound at a time: Rusty yelling at me, stirring her coffee, a teaspoon tossed into the sink, Rusty slamming the door. She, in her frustration, spurred by dictates of a raging heart, accused me of many things; things she soon learned were not only hurtful but impossible to prove.

She rarely acted the jilted lover, and when she did, it was more out of utter frustration than premeditated revenge. I, when the cotton wool blocked out the world, drawing me into a warm expansive void, sunk to the deepest ocean floors of feeling. Rusty never understood the solitude rituals and, feeling rejected, accused me of sadistic tendencies. She refused to accept that she deserved better than me, and hung on even when I could not sustain even simple conversations. I trained my ears to ignore the city ambience, to pick up the faintest sounds: mosquitoes wheezing overhead, water dripping into drainpipes, the wind whistling against twigs. A liberating silence soon descended on me. It lasted a few hours at first, but deepened with each passing day, until Rusty stopped coming. She returned a few weeks later, angry and remorseful. We sat in silence: 'You are strange,' she said, to which I answered, 'I know,' and drifted back into my void of silence.

My near silence was nothing complicated: one day I, unplanned, simply woke up with little or nothing to say. A few words, so sparse that I might as well have opted for complete silence. It was hard convincing Rusty that my sudden economy with words had nothing to do with her, that to some extent it also had little to do with Columbus' selfless life, lived with humour and flair, concluded with the most beautiful and imaginative of funerals, a funeral that shunned grief, that illuminated the sensory secrets that make life more deserving than death. Columbus knew, in death, or in the anticipation of death, not to lose sight of the charms of quirky sensibilities. That is what I remembered him for: his belief in things off beat and obscure; how he dismissed a need for romantic love, yet fell hopelessly in love with CNN newsreaders, how he over-analysed breastfeeding literature even though he wanted no children, how he secretly meditated in solidarity with terminally ill strangers, how he found beauty and serenity in cemeteries.

I thought, people are conceived in all sorts of ways: LSD-induced intimacies after rock 'n' roll concerts; a reckless, handsome rock star on the prowl for foreign thrills; weirdos conceived on boardroom tables from penises of anaemic bosses, accidental lusts at hotel poolsides, affairs ignited in hospital waiting rooms, births from player cousins with midnight tip-toeing gifts, humans created from carnal blackmail (I'm going tell your husband you had two abortions, and let's see how you stay in that mansion); imbeciles conceived in an aircraft restroom at 30 000 feet, from the occasional skinny-dipping rituals; cripples born from sombre marriages, from the haze of narcotics, accidental conceptions from boredom and heartache, erotic privileges extended to colleagues for unknown reasons, karma punishing errant spouses, from one-night stands in foreign cities and beds; losers born from spiteful lovers bent on lifetime entrapments; saints born to pimpled adolescents discovering carnal surges in public restrooms; psychos conceived on the back seats of cars, in clubs; unwanted souls drifting around the earth in displeasure and angst. Which category, I thought to myself, best suited Columbus?

EUGENE WENTZEL

Columbus was nothing like his brother, Eugene, whom I erroneously dismissed as a mean-spirited toad. It soon dawned on me, though, that Eugene's tantrums and outbursts hid a fragile snail, whose shell was slowly cracking, threatening to expose helpless tenderness, tenderness poisoned by frustrations of suspect artistic talents, his rusty marriage to Boni, which as I could see, was hanging by a thread. Eugene's rebellion against all things authoritarian had not earned him friends or peace, for he had somehow managed to live outside of existence, convinced himself that his marriage could still work, that it should work, even after Boni caught him at The Rembrandt, his painting studio at the Braamfontein Gallery, fondling Marcus Bruno, his sculptor lover.

The discovery wounded Boni, who in her rage, swung a garden spade through the pride of Eugene's art collection, his depressing smudges of green and yellow oils on canvas that could as well have been paint spill accidents. When Pete found out, reliably told by a sobbing Boni, Eugene's shell was burst open, leaving him ill-mannered and temperamental. Boni told Pete that Eugene was a shadow, that all he lived for were the paint accidents he called paintings, that he was a 'selfish goat' with no notable achievements except his crude self-portraits and body odour.

It was after the Marcus incident that Boni went berserk: cursing and mocking him, hurling her stilettos in daring provocations, smashing through The Rembrandt with a garden spade whenever she pleased. Eugene seemed defenceless against Boni's callous theatrics, her seething displays of anger that bordered on criminality: 'You're ugly anyway!' she had exploded. 'I don't know what I ever saw in a leech like you, sharing my every cent, buying you anything and everything, from cigarettes to the clothes on your back!

'Even The Rembrandt is not truly yours. You inherited it. You survive on rent from talented, proper artists, without whom you are broke. What would you have become if it were not for your father and me? And this is how you reward me? You fuck other people? Other men! You're wrong if you think I care. Go on. Screw your pretty-boy Marcus. Romp until you both bleed and die. I trusted you, took you in when all you had was that ridiculous, mauve Mickey Mouse underwear with holes, you ungrateful swine of a fucking pig! I loved you, cherished your eyesores you call art, wasting paint and canvases with the offensive eyesores you call paintings. You conniving rattlesnake of a mediocre creature! Even I, a humble kindergarten teacher, have some purpose in life, some dignity.'

She would then pick up the garden spade, swinging it at everything in sight, leaving scattered debris: wooden fragments from painting frames, paint spurts from burst paint cans, Eugene's cheese and tomato sandwiches, plastic bits from his adored radio. She even chopped the head off *The Virgin Mary*, a gift of passion given to him by Marcus, who as Boni saw it, was Godless. I feared Boni was one day going to chop Eugene with that garden spade, how her weekly raids of The Rembrandt seemed like glances of horrors yet to come. Columbus and I were dumbstruck by it all, suspected nothing untoward about Marcus' late-evening visits to The Rembrandt.

Not even I, the keen observer, sensed that Eugene's borderline madness hid such explosive domestic turmoil, that what seemed like his permanent irritation masked suppressed rage against Boni's equally determined attacks. It was impossible to determine where Eugene's crimes began and ended: if it was because he lacked ambition, or the affair he had with Marcus, his being secretly gay, or simply being ugly (which should never be a crime), or because he had no artistic talent whatsoever.

So what if he dropped out of a Sports Management degree only a week into the first semester? So what if he decided after two long years of fanatical commitment that motor racing was too dangerous for him, or given up on three morose years as a long-faced barber in Orange Grove? Or the barren three years spent as a pliant, talentless student of the flute with the Johannesburg Philharmonic Orchestra? Eugene quarrelled with everyone: with Columbus and Pete, his driving and flute instructors, agitated clients who insisted on particular haircuts and not what he thought suited them better. A brawl with such a client, protesting against too experimental a haircut, earned Eugene two years' imprisonment, for which he was released early (one year and two months) for good behaviour.

It was at the Sun City penitentiary that the first artistic spark was ignited, him seeing breathtaking portraits and landscapes by rapists and fraudsters. It was after his release, aged 38, that he pleaded with Pete for permission to oversee the family art gallery. Pete declined to hear another word from Eugene, only relenting following Eugene's unlikely but plausible suicide threats. It was more getting him off his back and avoiding Eugene's embarrassing visits to Chris Hani High that he was given an early inheritance; a desperately needed lifeline, a small but sizeable portion from the Wentzel family cents invested over 37 years in Forge Ahead Capital. He renamed Braamfontein Art Gallery The Rembrandt, renting out the unused gallery space to promising artists — artists who had sold-out exhibitions, whose paintings adorned the boardrooms of Infinity Bank and Touchstone Attorneys. Eugene resented these artists, who — renting a portion of his inheritance — outsold him at every turn. It saddened him that their success seemed so effortless, enjoyable even, while his crack-of-dawn and midnight toils yielded little by way of sales or anything resembling recognition.

So he turned to the bottle, painted while gulping red wine straight from the bottle. This annoyed me; I have no time for self-pitying drunkards. It was Boni who bought some of his paintings, which she saw as lifetime loans designed to fill Eugene's financial craters, the gloomy weeks between the 15th and 30th of the month; when Eugene had exhausted his rent earnings from the previous month, some of which he later confessed to horse betting and showering Marcus with expensive French fragrances. Boni had her suspicions, but dismissed the gnawing angst of an absent-present husband-lover. She herself had unexploded mortars from her failed marriage to Armand, a promising pilot, who crashed his rented Mark II over restricted military space, lost his pilot licence, then developed a concerning taste for violence. God! I despaired at the time, why couldn't I meet or hear of normal, functioning people? While I loved Columbus, our friendship somehow meant exposure to alarming things, tentacles to shady persons and their histories, tentacles that seemed to know no boundaries to their reach.

When Eugene had met Boni at an art shop in Killarney Mall, Johannesburg, neither of them could have possibly known they would end up sharing a flat in the seedy suburb of Orange Grove. Neither would have predicted that Eugene would live on the edge, become a rebellious cynic living on his father's handouts, his pity, his parental obligations. Neither would have known their hesitant courtship in Orange Grove would wholly be funded by his father's irritation, his desire to contain Eugene's lack of ambition, his remorseless abuse of his father's goodwill. The last straw came when Eugene missed Kate's funeral. Boni said she had reported him missing, only for Eugene to crawl out of an ancient Volkswagen Passat, drunk as a bat, his eyes bloodshot from a week of touring Johannesburg clubs with The Grenades, his newfound fellow drunks masquerading as musicians, a 'band'. When he finally made it to Dr Coetzee's palace of a house in Houghton – in Boni's temperamental Mazda, an old birthday present that choked them with petrol fumes, blurred their vision with its yellowing windshield, woke them at ungodly hours with its unreliable alarm – Eugene was shown a Chinese vase, inside which were Kate's ashes.

Eugene knew of his mother's obsession with plastic surgery, of the many times she raided the Internet for case studies, but instead his rebellion led him to The Grenades the day Kate made the fatal decision to defy a paunchy stomach, assaulted by two pregnancies, leaving it flabby and sensually repulsive. Eugene was the only person we knew who could shrug off grief, who could with shoulders raised and hands thrown in the air, conclude: 'People die. Even mothers. Sucks. But, hey, its life.' Then tears. More tears. Hisses. Snot. Deep sighs. Wounded chuckles. Then silence.

COLUMBUS
WENTZEL

The university sat on a hill, a deceptively elevated Braamfontein point hidden by jacarandas and haphazard city architecture, an ambience swarming with Campus Tribes: The Niggers with their phoney American accents, The Nerds with their antisocial ways, The Sporty Types with their sweaty toils, The Social Misfits accused of being underwear thieves, the Biblical Types dripping with biblical cautions, The Spoilt Brats dropped off in BMWs the size of ocean liners, The Campus Sluts with their promiscuous cathedrals, The Arty Souls with their dreadlocks and peculiar body ornaments, The Thinkers with their Plato and Aristotle quotations, esteemed members of Alcoholics Anonymous, The Party Animals with their eternal celebrations, Pseudo Politicians with their stillborn revolutions, The Drifters belonging to none of the others, Church Choirs and Bible Study mobs: Herolds and Monicas who aspired for high political office, Margarets and Zoës who would one day own psychiatric practices, Thembas and Xoliswas who would become fund managers, Cocos and Elizabeths who would someday rewrite constitutions of republics, Amandas and Williams destined to find cures to dread disease. There were also Franks and

RUSTY BELL

Patricks who were ordained to tumultuous marriages and dishonest lives.

The Pseudo Politicians in the Political Tribe staged Bad Food Marches and protests, but were persuaded by the realities of hunger to 'fight the revolution from within the dining hall', thus succumbing to, like the rest of us, the watery yellow paste that was supposed to be eggs, jaw-breaking steak that often tasted like an old shoe dipped in sauce, and coffee meant to service campus hordes rather than fine percolation concerns of baristas.

* * *

Because he stayed off campus, with his tortured brother Eugene and Eugene's sweetheart Boni, in Orange Grove, Columbus missed out on happenings on campus, the lightning bolt that was Rusty Bell. Few things compared to the little pleasures of secretly observing her busy with mundane things: clipping toenails, drying clothes in the laundry room, peeling an orange. She never said a word to anyone, which made her magical, surreal even. Not that it was completely impossible to probe, to from a position of anonymity, silently establish the four-digit extension number allocated to Room 308 at David Webster Hall.

The problem was never securing Rusty Bell's number, but what to say the moment she picked up the phone. There were confirmed rumours that she never answered internal calls, only scheduled calls from home. The only other option was anonymous notes slid under her door. She saw them, and tossed them into the corridor garbage bin after reading. The bin became a fishing spot for rejected love overtures, heaped amid discarded shampoo bottles, lecture notes and stale bread.

I befriended Columbus on condition that he refrain from cannabis, to which he, tongue-in-cheek, answered, 'You cheeky little shit. Not a chance in hell.' It was a daring insult, executed with breathtaking composure. I told Columbus of my predicament: Rusty Bell. That is how we became friends, how Columbus got to know of my aborted attempts to phone her. Columbus, in his cerebral manner, said, 'A whole residence full of idiots. Can't you Einsteins figure out that the girl unplugs her phone? That none of your traumas get to her? A girl like you describe is clever. You have to always think five steps ahead. Evoke the unexpected. Accuse her of things, unsettle her, make her want to defend herself. Corner her with unexpected admonishing, but include some open-ended compliments.

'She has to want to hear, to know more. Not an avalanche of desperate phone calls. That's too predictable, too ordinary. Be a sophisticated nuisance: that way you learn her boundaries; measure the range of her defences. Slow things down. See and understand details. That is how you will get her attention – but not necessarily her affections, of course. Wars are won one battle at a time. Say she hates pitiful characters. Won't all your grovelling nauseate her? One more thing . . . Girls like that know what they're about, so you have to somehow make her believe you're seeing the world as she would, that you're worthy of her attention. That you'll complement her. You have to be willing to fail. Courage. Pretend you know what you're doing. Oh, and by the way, Rusty, whoever she is, already knows all you bastards want her. She can smell you, hopeless hunters, from hundreds of miles away.'

RUSTY BELL

He was sympathetic, said it is coded in nature that courting is fraught with rebukes, even bruises. There are hundreds of examples on the National Geographic channel. It's all laid bare: zebras tolerating kicks, polar bears walking for hundreds of kilometres, lions tearing each other to shreds. In other words, Rusty was merely following the rules of nature. I took Columbus' advice: slowed everything down. A pattern soon crystallised. Rusty walked from late lectures on her lonesome on Mondays and Thursdays. I imagined it would be tedious learning about incisors and root canals – knew I had to conceive an intricate 'surprise and capture' (Columbus' words) manoeuvre. It sounded to me like I had to be some kind of mounted cattle ranger, that romance was squeezed out of the whole saga. So I abandoned my plot as too risky. I knew that a hundred other plots were being thought and refined – for Rusty somehow, like a cowboy, rode us through deep rivers, jabbed her spurs into our collective ribs. How we neighed and purred to her silent commands. Poor horses.

* * *

I dialled Rusty's extension number: 0448 – and braced myself for all manner of abuse. It rang for a long time, until a sleepy, faint voice said: 'Hello, Rusty. Please call in five hours.' 'Sure. It's Michael in Room GO77,' said I. I heard a faint yawn, and gently hung up. Five hours meant midnight. I set every alarm within reach to wake me at ten, for a shower. But the plan fell apart. My phone rang at 11.55 p.m., and an obviously drunk Kerusha (a veteran of the History of Art class, who changed courses every semester) on the other side of the line said she was not wearing any panties. 'There is absolutely nothing wrong with fresh air, Kerusha Maharaj,' I answered. 'But what does that have to do with me?' Kerusha burst into tears, at exactly the same time someone knocked at my door, rendering my poetic verse, my earlier composure, redundant.

I opened the door expecting to see some fool in underpants in pursuit of sugar or tea bags, not Rusty Bell in person. It was terrifying. Disarming. Overwhelming. 'I thought I was going to call you at midnight?' I said offering her a seat. 'I am all ears,' she said sitting, a posture of a seasoned diplomat rather than a dental student. 'You wanted to talk to me?'

'Yes.'

'What about?'

That was the moment I wanted to say: 'Tell me something, Rusty Bell, what colour are your nipples?' Instead, I said, 'Have you heard of a gentleman called Jon Bon Jovi?'

'Jovi who? You are not serious?'

'I am. He . . .'

'Excuse me . . . And you are?'

'Michael.'

'Mr Awkward. I know who you are. Are we done then?'

'Depends entirely on you. Dental student. Beautiful. Wealthy family. Dreadful public image. I would say there is a lot to talk about?'

'Such as?'

'My dilemma.'

'You have a dilemma?'

'Yes and no.'

'Explain.'

'Yes, because I am curious if you would, in your underwear, share a shower with me, or if you prefer the thrills of the bathtub. No, because I am concerned, not worried, that you will think me a freak and call campus security.'

She blushed. 'I am not about to discuss my bathing habits with a total stranger.'

'No disrespect, but undergarments are overrated.' I countered.

'Seriously, now. Who *are* you?'

'Some fool, born and bred in Alexandra, wrestling Corporate Law, a bit of Art History. I think I am in love, maybe infatuated by a yet-to-be-confirmed reclusive snob.'

'Would that be me?'

'Indeed.'

Rusty burst out laughing. She had black gums. She cupped her mouth to stifle her raucous laughter. 'Is that your best bait?'

'No. I also have some rat poison, if you don't cooperate.' She shook her head in pleasure and disbelief. Pleasure from a conversation swarming with minute love detonations.

'Rat poison?'

'Yes. Failing which I have to steal all your clothes, torch your room so that you flee from the flames in the nude.'

'I don't sleep naked.'

'I said nothing about naked.'

'You said nude.'

'But nude is not naked. There is artistry, a grace to nudity. Naked suggests there is something wrong.'

'Is that what they teach you in History of Art?'

'No. They teach no such things.'

'What then? What do they teach?'

'Well, dead artists who created famous artworks.'

'Masterpieces?'

'Some of them, yes.'

'You have a favourite?'

'No.'

'Why not?'

'I live in the present, among the living.'

Rusty cracked up: 'You're a very sick person. Are you sure you haven't escaped from some madhouse?'

'I have, but don't tell anyone,' I whispered.

'Law, History of Art of all things?'

'Why not?'

'Well, I would have thought South Africa needs more economists, doctors?'

'But I am a doctor. Art and Law are medicine for all manner of injustices.'

'I mean a real doctor. Like heal asthma and hypertension – that kind of doctor.'

'You're a dentist in waiting, so you'll kill poor asthma and hypertension patients if you dared to treat them. Your science is limited to teeth. How exactly are we so different?'

'You are so full of it. I am a dental surgeon in the making. Not just a dentist.'

'Good. I am a capable scholar of the law, learning how to nudge people into the habits of justice.'

RUSTY BELL

'Ambitious,' she said.
'Yes. But aren't all great things?'
'Maybe.'
'I have to go to bed now, Mr Law Scholar. See you around.'
'Likewise.'

I was too touched not to be tearful. I, emboldened by her visit, her laughter, her assessment that I had lunatic credentials, decided not to ask her about Bon Jovi the next time we met, but to ask the *real* question that plagued me, the answer to which was, as already said, 'Honey-brown.'

* * *

Rusty Bell was a more-than-capable debater. I never knew when she would turn the tables, corner me with overwhelming facts. Once a week, mostly at the stroke of midnight, Rusty, knocked at my door. We spoke, laughed, argued and reflected on all things under the sun: world poverty, how sugar daddies preyed on willing campus sluts, sexual exhibitionism in America and now South African music videos. Our sudden friendship blossomed into strolls around campus, to the fury and detriment of her multitude of hibernating suitors. I cannot say I did not enjoy basking in that glory, of being chosen. Those midnight visits took a toll on my sleeping patterns, but the inconvenience of sleep was nothing compared to the bliss of seeing her throw her head back in unguarded laughter. It was during those visits that we drifted into affectionate silences, that we resisted a magnetic desire to kiss. So we kissed on the cheeks, like gangstas, conscious of the itch that got redder by the day. She, months later, developed audacious wishes: that I check her breasts for cancer lumps, for an opinion on a tattoo in a provocative place (the inner upper thigh – she wore an acceptable mini skirt and immodest silk underwear), a night in my bed whenever she was at the mercy of period pains.

As much as we knew we were playing with a live grenade, the pending moment for looming wild indiscretions, we also knew that would taint our atypical amusements. It always felt out of place, incestuous even, every time we almost caved into desire. Besides being tempted by Rusty's elaborate sensuality, I resolved to live with my raging nocturnal hungers, my self-inflicted depravations.

But how – amid such rampant fornication, new-found and abundant campus freedoms, away from glaring prison walls of mothers, fathers and religion – was it possible that we could uphold such brittle chastity? It seemed like the seventies all over again, only without the rock 'n' roll, without such promiscuity being synonymous with Aids and ruin. It was then that I figured there was never such a thing as the History of Art. It was, quite alarmingly, within the walls of David Webster Hall that I observed the foundations of adult life: lessons in deception, accidental pregnancies and abortions, flexible romantic thrills without the traumas of marriage.

The sum total of all the triumphs and frustrations of later life seemed to me born out of the pursuit of the true self – an opinion of oneself – while at the same time conforming to the smirks and valour of intentional campus cruelties: hunting Rusty Bells come rain or shine, bedding ugly lovesick girls and later accusing, dismissing them of being ambitious stalkers. I submitted a paper on this, 'The History of Life', for which I dethroned Columbus with an unheard-of 95 per cent.

To fortify my defences against the inevitable, the gangsta kisses that would ultimately evolve into other things, I introduced Rusty Bell to Columbus at a *Schindler's List* screening at the School of Drama. That was the day Columbus, laughing as always, disclosed his medically induced hepatitis diagnosis. It was only weeks later, with Rusty Bell now firmly the matriarch of The Triumvirate, that we knew Columbus would require surgery, an organ donor.

He, Columbus, correctly predicted, 'Death comes in a million guises.' He was not, as Rusty Bell and I had expected, killed by tragedies of the liver.

* * *

I met Christopher Wentzel – handsome, with curly brown hair and tearful ocean-blue eyes – in a History of Art class. It was inevitable that we would be friends, that it would be a perfect friendship, ruined by laughter, by minor perversities of the mind. I, out of fondness and fooling around, pet named him Columbus. We debated everything. Dali's molten and deformed watches. Modigliani's *Reclining Nude*. That sly Mona Lisa smile. Kentridge. Noria Mabasa. It was remarkable how Columbus could sit through an entire semester without a whisper, and then shock everyone with a single penetrating comment. All of art, Columbus once said, with the exception of a few unrelated artworks, in some way celebrates the beauty of the human body – particularly the nude woman. Artists, he argued, are obsessed with capturing longing and desire and, in their fantasies, capture naked beings in wood, stone and iron. On canvas. Art, according to Mr Wentzel, was the sum total of human depravations. I had never seen Professor Mbembe so elated, so agreeable, so exalted. So agreeable that he declared the course 'The History of Human Depravations'. Columbus was quick to add, not without Professor Mbembe grinning from ear to ear, that it was 'The History of Measured Human Depravations And Excesses And All The Splendour In Between'.

* * *

Rusty and I visited Columbus at Eugene's apartment on Louis Botha Avenue, Orange Grove. He was horsing around as usual, said he was tired of lectures on dead artists of 'meagre' talents. He laughed until he collapsed, clutching his chest. I thought Columbus was clowning around, pulling faces, until paramedics, half an hour later, solemnly declared the unthinkable.

Medically, explained the paramedic, it is rare but indeed possible to die from laughter. Cardiac arrest. It is possible that Columbus had, unbeknown to him, problems with his heart.

He would have, if he had lived a few minutes longer, known the purpose of our visit. He would have been pleased at the news of being elected godfather to our seedling; Rusty intended conceiving on the dentist's chair, amid bloody cotton wool and needles in a trash basket – remnants of extracted rusting molars. His death certificate, according to Pete, said Columbus succumbed to natural causes. Laughter seemed too morbid an excuse for such a solemn incident. A story waited our friends of the future: we had a friend we called Columbus. He was killed by laughter.

* * *

Columbus had, in life, had his funeral wishes written down, detailed instructions deposited in a safety deposit box at Spencer & Young Inc., the Wentzel family attorneys on Twelfth Street, Melville. I had had the honour of assisting Pete in the interpretation of some of the peculiarities: in other words, advising him which of Columbus' instructions could be omitted, without it being grossly offensive to the deceased. 'C. Wentzel Funeral Commandments' was a detailed list, typed on a typewriter, with perfect punctuation.

The perfectionist in him – the part of him that refused to allow him to simply surrender – ensured that not only were his Commandments legible, but he also took the trouble of attaching a separate page with explanatory notes: how to interpret, understand and administer the Commandments. The separate page, also neatly typed in single spacing, included explicit task allocations to specific individuals and a list of substitute persons in the event that delegated people were unavailable. It was, therefore, not by accident that Professor Mbembe gave a moving eulogy and Zubeida Patel from the History of Art class read the cards attached to the wreaths, while I was left alone to simply mourn. Columbus' instruction ensured that this was crystal clear: 'My dear friend should be left alone to mourn.' So this is exactly what I did by the graveside. Between my repressed sobs, I greatly admired Columbus' foresight, that not even death clouded his meticulous planning, so thoughtful that it took into account even the dreary and depressing dramas of death and burials. It was an unfunereal occasion. Columbus had, years before his death, reflected on the exact details of his funeral: the polished mahogany casket, the tulips in clay pots at the foot of the grave, the twelve white pigeons that were to be released at exactly fifteen minutes before midnight, as well as the custard and the pineapple jelly that was to be served by the graveside, failing which mourners were to be served strawberries and cream.

Columbus insisted, in capital letters, that funeral hymns were completely off limits, that the only scripture permitted was The Song of Solomon. It was a sensual funeral, full of memorable charms that chiselled the grief from our collective bosoms. The week of the funeral was brimming with memories of him – stories of love and kindness: how he bought heaters for old-age homes, spend hours at Christ The King Care Centre, his bottomless patience with lazy freshmen who attended his History of Art tutorials, his generosity with his limited finances.

It was proper that our hearts bled, sank with the purplish-brown casket, to the meditative grooves of Bon Jovi, playing 'Something to Believe In'. I remember the funeral, all two hours, as a painful blur of mourners in their pyjamas, each clutching a lit candle, resulting in a half-sombre event that from a distance resembled a mute rock concert. This was consistent with Columbus' Commandment 8, which clearly stated: 'Bury me in the evening, under glittering stars from above and a sea of lit candles from among yourselves.' Commandment 7 was Columbus at his best: 'For those who understandably feel the urge to weep, please do so with some level of composure.' The lunatic in him then concluded, still under Commandment 7, 'Like all things under the sun, composure is relative. So howl your lungs out if so moved by the tragedy of my passing (till we meet again), but please don't forget the strawberries in your howling; they are there for your sensual delight.'

Professor Mbembe read The Commandments out loud. We giggled. Laughed. Sobbed. Ate strawberries. Licked cream off our quivering lips. It was a delightful, memorable evening, devoid of grief, sorrows that make funerals sombre, weepy things. Columbus had, with ten brief requests, ensured posthumous presence of his peculiar mind — we, in our pyjamas, fobbing off moths, which somehow understood the gravity of our collective mourning and descended on the candles with moderate and guarded interest, a cautious display of insect empathy.

Commandment 4 explicitly forbade the use of anything remotely resembling a motorised hearse, instructing that the casket be pulled by a single white horse. That horse, with its iron shoes clacking across the tarmac, with its twitchy tail and twitchy nostrils, street lights along Jorissen Street bouncing off the polished casket, the clay pots with their tulips, the strawberries and bowls of cream, the unlit candles, the coy pigeons in their temporary cages, constellations of stars above seen from under and through cemetery tree branches, the modest cortège (family and close friends) in pyjamas walked into the Braamfontein Cemetery wherein the silence was made molten by ACDC riffs, where I saw Zubeida Patel's beautiful collarbones lit by her candle, her dimples encouraging inappropriate thoughts. This — all of this — taught me that funerals did not have to be depressing, that with the right measure of madness, funerals had the potential to be light-hearted and enjoyable things.

Only Columbus could manage such a twisted view of existence, only he could, even in death, pour onto life bucketfuls of pranks. That is why I loved him: for his madness. One last detail about the funeral: when the pigeons were freed, fluttering in the late night, I in my mind's eye saw my friend at the Heavenly Gates Undertakers, lying cold on a stretcher: calm, rigid, in a soulless, handsome, refrigerated kind of way. It was only when Alfred, a bow-legged and aged mortician, replaced the white sheet that covered Columbus that the post-mortem scars bared their ugliness. My friend: butchered and sewn, like an old shoe. It was then that I caught sight of something unlike Columbus: a golden brown nest of curly, rich-textured pubic hair. Cheeky, this discovery, for Columbus had in life been an exemplary custodian of male grooming – which I erroneously concluded would include manicured carnal gardens. That unfortunate oversight aside, Columbus was a charmer of the finest breed, a rare specimen. Intense. Sobering. Of peculiar thoughts.

* * *

I secretly made up my mind that, though besotted with Rusty's beautiful navel, her ferocious intellect, all her sleep-talking about red tractors and aeroplane crashes in sunflower fields, it was impossible for the me of the future – post our seemingly concluded forthcoming marriage – to have her parents as my in-laws. How was it that her mother, Catherine, pretty and rumoured to be an efficient nurse, interesting in parts, awkward with her five-minute hugs (her breasts were, for someone her age, 58, mysteriously firm and too warm for comfort) would allow herself to be bullied, silenced and generally disregarded by that pot-bellied tyrant of a husband with big ears, bad skin and vice-like handshakes?

How did she put up with his autocratic and suspicious ways? Did she have to defer to him even on the simplest, most pointless details? 'Will Papa appreciate a foot rub? Does Papa fancy a long or short visit? How is Papa's ingrown toenail now?' For her trouble, Catherine only ever got half-groans, heavy breathing and blank stares from Abednego.

For his arrogance and tyrannical tendencies, I, in my quiet reflections, made it clear – by deed rather than word – to Abednego that I was unwilling to be a scared mouse around him. I was forthright with Rusty: 'Your father,' I said, 'is a malicious swine.' She was shocked, not sure whether to laugh or cry. I empathised. But that did not change my opinion of Abednego. I still thought he was a swine, the way he treated Catherine.

I, with Rusty sleep-talking about one-legged dogs and balloons in swimming pools, thought about Pete and Kate, about Abednego and Catherine, Rusty and I. I concluded that marriage could be purgatorial, a cage crawling with ingrown toenails and foot rubs, festering with silent judgements that made life almost unbearable. Of grave concern was Rusty's misguided complicity when it came to Abednego's excesses, how she as an only child saw nothing wrong in being indifferent. Did she expect me to, like Catherine, be a hound on a leash? What did she make of Abednego's unsolicited lectures to me: on sacrifice and good moral standing, his storm of questions: what did my parents do, what church I went to, what did I plan to do with my life, had anyone in my family been to prison, for what offences, where were they now and what were they doing with their lives, did I believe in God, why or why not, was anyone born out of wedlock in my family tree, any peculiar deaths or cases of mental instability – until Catherine, for the very first time, cautiously said: 'Would you like a back rub, Papa? I am sure Michael won't have answers to all your questions.' Abednego simply groaned, and stood up to leave.

CONSULTATION TWELVE

I confused the dates and times for my twelfth consultation. Dr West had indicated be would be travelling (a visit to that Spaniard, the head doctor? I dared to surmise) during the week of 8 March. It was only when Audrey answered the buzz of the intercom that the she reminded me that Dr West was away. But she invited me in, requested that I pardon the mess caused by her rearranging Dr West's filing system. I have to confess that I, when not unravelling the conundrums of philosophy, thought about Audrey sometimes, allowed myself to imagine certain pleasure, liberties. Unsure, vulnerable, yet real possibilities. She wore a black mini dress, a brilliantly tailored gem of a garment with trimmings and openings in the right places: polka-dot collar, a discreet slit over the right thigh, a giant red button that secured the dress over her remarkable neck. A deep-red cardigan took care of the upper torso and, her red-soled stilettos lay neatly next to one of the couches.

She walked barefoot, thoughtfully, from one filing cabinet to the next. Gorgeous legs. A devastating profile. Those pouty lips, begging to be kissed. She mouthed alphabets, mentally arranging surnames of patients. She was, strangely, pleased to see me – all that blushing, the coy yet deliberate glances. Her toenails could have done with a fresh coat of nail polish – a revival of the purplish shade in various stages of peeling off. She offered me a seat, Dr West's chair, the throne from which he deciphered human tragedies, from which he patiently asked questions with discreet judgements, from which he had to think ahead, predict how to deal with unexpected meltdowns. It was from that chair that Dr West blended into the background, seemed insignificant, the master of weighing up emotional pauses.

His choice of interior decor had ensured witnesses to his theatre of sobs and hisses: pictures of Bill Clinton surrounded by a group of singing children in Uganda, Gabriel Márquez receiving the Nobel Prize, a jubilant Idi Amin in full Scottish regalia, Mandela sewing on Robben Island, a shot of John Kennedy saluting JFK's horse-drawn coffin, that Kevin Carter image of a vulture stalking a starving child. It dawned on me that each picture, no doubt carefully selected, said something (not quite sure what) about existence. And what perplexing juxtapositions!

Audrey opened and sealed boxes, discarded out-of-date psychology journals, continued mouthing letters of the alphabet: J. Cromwell, D. Dikobe, Z. Maharaj, P. Woodhouse. I, in an effort to seem at ease, helped myself to dried mangoes, on which Audrey nibbled between her filing.

'I better get going,' I said. She looked up, a typed report with red pen underlining in her hand, and said, 'I won't die if you stay.'

'Meaning?'

'Stay.'

'Well, isn't it inappropriate, with all these secrets scattered around the consultation room?'

'Says who?'

'Well, doctor-patient confidentiality?'

'Here. John Cromwell: filthy as a practising paedophile ever gets. Preyed on two-year-olds.'

'Audrey!'

'Audrey what? Some of these psychos are either languishing in jail or dead.'

'What will Dr West think?'

'Nothing. D'you really think he walks around agonising about deviants who fuck watermelons, pathological liars who defraud orphanages, alcoholics who butchered their wives? Is that what you think: that Kevin lives his life cringing and wincing at every blot contained in these files?' She picked up the files, pulled out Dr West's meticulous notes: 'Let's see . . . What have we here? Amanda Dube, a prostitute who found and lost and found Jesus, Elizabeth Reed drowned her twin daughters to spite a philandering boyfriend, and Colonel Maritz, a Vlakplaas kingpin, specialising in making blacks disappear without trace. These files, all 500 of them, contain the most hideous, most depraved and ruthless tales you can ever imagine. D'you think Kevin kisses his children goodbye at the school gates thinking of all the rot in these patient files? Most of these horrors are perfectly normal and capable people simply being full of it. Granted, there are some – a small percentage – who genuinely need help and affirmation, but the rest are fuckheads abusing their good medical insurance, drowning in self-pity and guilt.'

She smiled, transferred prearranged blue and yellow files into filing cabinets, all the while double-checking the alphabetical sequence. Those calves of hers. Those small, efficient hands. The small wristwatch she says was a gift from an ex-boyfriend, 'a perfectly capable, marriage-averse type, a software programmer with a zero attention span. Besides his computer codes, really shocking lack of concentration. Sleep-with-shoes-on kind of delinquency . . .'

Genius? 'Oh, yes.'

Looks? 'Double tick.'

Style? 'Spades full.'

Money? 'Bank vaults. Father's a controlling shareholder of East Platinum, so the Smiths defrost their refrigerators onto bank notes.'

Bedroom antics? 'That's private. And, let's see: Dependability? Zero. Bucketfuls of culinary skills. Cooks sinfully good meals. And here I am, rearranging confessions from fucking Cromwell – God, he's a dick! – and other delusional, depraved creatures of his ilk.'

One hour, and the files were neatly in their respective filing cabinets, leaving Audrey to polish furniture and empty the trash basket of its negligible contents: a twisted paperclip, shredded documents, a perfume box. I knew without asking that Audrey had read my file, though she downplayed her prying eyes by volunteering stories about Cromwells. I also knew there was something very special about Audrey, something feminine, carefree, something profound – complex even – in how she switched from one topic to the next with breathtaking agility, how she could discuss paedophiles and boyfriends and Dr West in one passionate conversation, a conversation that lingered long after she had moved on with her tasks. She was interesting, hiding her true self, a self far removed from the obedient and efficient PA serving bottled water and dried fruit to psychopaths.

    Dr West had, unbeknown to either Audrey or me, never left for Spain. This was the reason I felt safe to will pleasure into being. My hand travelled halfway up Audrey's thigh, almost all the way, inches short of her humid horizons. My fingers transmitted oppressive sensations, while my eyes crept through the giant red button of her dress, where a pair of turgid breasts guarded her muted sighs. I lifted her onto Dr West's desk, stood between her slightly parted legs, fed on her lip-glossed, pouty lips, lips that tasted like strawberries – only with citrus undertones. It seemed the longest seven minutes I ever imagined possible, during which Audrey saw, over my shoulder, Dr West staring in absolute horror. We composed ourselves, acknowledged it had to end, that all seven minutes had to be forgotten. But we also (on the telephone later) agreed that life would have been explosive had we entered the eighth minute, and every other minute thereafter. How could I explain this to Dr West: strawberry lips with citrus undertones? I would be accused of remorselessness. Loathed. Condemned. I would be crucified for a seven-minute affair, for twelve seconds of weakness; for three seconds of letting my hand wander under Audrey's dress. I thought of Audrey Adams, whom I had, technically speaking, not bedded. How would Dr West weigh the conclusiveness of my intentions – if I would have indeed let my hand travel the remaining sprint to her forbidden spheres? I tossed and turned that evening, stared at the ceiling, plotted and raged and despaired – mostly at how Dr West seemed to enjoy punishment by silence, how he simply walked away.

* * *

The Audrey mishap aside, there were moments of untold tranquillity on Dr West's couch, of profound introspection and inner peace. I was making steady progress, he assured me, but I was not yet out of the woods. It was during my eighteenth visit that Dr West let me in on the deceptions of PTS. Since our furtive encounter, Audrey pretended to not see me, and went about her PA rituals without as much as a whisper, except for a brief nod that could have been a greeting.

'PTS,' continued Dr West, 'is essentially a belated response to traumatic environments or incidents. Proper and early diagnosis goes a long way in limiting damaging outcomes.'

'And PTS is?'

'Post-traumatic stress. How are we doing with sleep these days?'

'On and off.'

'Nightmares?'

'None so far.'

'Columbus dreams?'

'None. Just memories.'

'Such as?'

'Columbus and I debated masterpieces. Sekoto. Mabasa. Modigliani. Not even resting my head on Rusty's supremely sculptured breasts, her honey-brown buttons massaging my ear lobes, compared to the calm I felt talking to Columbus.'

'And the cat visitor, cat with a bowtie? Do you still believe cats can tell stories?'

'Yes. I'm convinced the cat is real. That he spoke.'

Dr West shuffled in his chair. 'And the Rusty issues?'

'Tragically and predictably purgatorial.'

'That bad?'

'Yes. That long, lyrical email of wanting to be loved and groped and what not. So I told her to move on with her life. I can't have her put a leash on me.'

'She accepted?'

'Predictably, no. She threatened to kill herself. But I have had enough death around me in the last year or so. Kate. Columbus. Pete. Now her?'

'You mentioned you read. Do you find pleasure in books?'

'Sometimes.'

'What are you reading now?'

'Nietzsche. Blaise Pascal.'

Dr West frowned, smiled broadly. 'Impressive.'

I was falling asleep, and I almost did not hear him, so my 'Thank you' was belated, marking the end of the session. Rusty's lyrical email of wanting to be loved and groped and what not read thus:

From: RustyBell@campus.ac.za
To: Michael@campus.ac.za
Subject: I am Sad

My Archangel Michael,

I don't know how to tell you this without sounding like a complete nutcase. But I am sad. Very sad. I never meant to compete with the memory of our dead friend. I just felt neglected. I understand that

Christopher meant a lot to you, that your brooding and starving yourself (eleven-day fasts, Michael!) is something I must learn to respect and understand, though I still think it's a bit extreme.

Anyway, I'm not sure if it means you have given up on me, on us, completely completely, as in no-chance-in-hell sort of thing. Anyway, I love talking to you, smelling you, and apologise for so badly wishing you to think of me (as if already your wife!) before we had even dated – you know, being lovers as opposed to being friends with access to things, things that would have otherwise been private. I know I can be temperamental and a bit of a control freak, something my mother says will never work with a thinker boyfriend. Mom says you're a thinker. I agree.

I just want you to share your thoughts, so I can get to know you better. About the suicide thing: it was stupid and insensitive. It'll never happen again. I am still upset that you think my father is a swine. I know he can be difficult and cold. But swine? Think about it, Michael. We have just over a year before graduation. Maybe we should use the time to get to know each other better. To correct mistakes. I bought new underwear today. I would like to show you, if you're keen. I have no lectures for the rest of today. Some love, bit of groping. So, I will let you have me (fuck sounds so obscene!), if you want. Let me know what you think?

Your Lover Friend, Rusty Bell

* * *

From: Michael@campus.ac.za
To: RustyBell@campus.ac.za
Subject: The Swine & Related Matters

Hi Rusty,
I am sad you are sad. I am also, within limits, ashamed of myself for calling your father that unpleasant word. I meant no harm; I just think he should treat your mother better. I think you're a great woman, and I know you are going to make someone very happy one day. But knowing myself the way I do, I foresee turmoil and unhappiness in times to come. I suggest we remain friends, as my feelings for you seem to me more brotherly rather than eros-esque (of the romantic, love kind). This is the only reason I was overcautious with our intimate moment – for I did not want to see you hurt.

The suicide thing: all forgiven, water under the bridge. My 'depression' has not helped things either, so I apologise for my withdrawals. Let's treat that issue as a private matter, for the obvious hurt it might cause. You deserve undivided attention and, I'm not sure I'm able to fully grant you the attention things of this nature demand. Advice taken on the starvation front. Your new undergarments: sounds terrific, tempted to see them, but it would be inappropriate. You have my friendship and respect to eternity.
Michael

* * *

I immersed myself in Nietzsche, in Pascal, fasted for another eleven days straight. 'Thought constitutes man's greatness,' said Pascal. I, light-headed from self-imposed starvation, made connections between diverse and intimate observations — covering vast landscapes of human triumphs and tragedies: Thought. Time. Madmen. Wretchedness. I, in my dreamlike state, with Nietzsche for company, travelled the furthest journey to the frontiers of the mind, Nietzsche's thoughts falling like snow from starry nights blanketing desolate deserts. Thoughts about passions. Nature. Deep comprehension. My excavations left me fatigued, yet thrilled at my accidental discovery of rumination and reflection.

A void echoed. It lulled unsuspecting Campus Tribes into corrosive slumber, slumber so deceptive that it sparked a crippled existence, parroting of dead and dying people's wisdoms. In residence meetings the Political Tribe assembled and impressed novices: they quoted Karl Marx and Dr King to rebel against suspect cafeteria eggs, to remind the Du Toits and Krugers of their contributions to human misery, but also as indirect intellectual charms into the beds of girls. But their revolution never seemed to get anywhere. It proved to be little more than an insurrection for pranksters, for bored snobs with too much time and meek purpose, a revolution that changed colours for no known reason, a rebellion allergic to sacrifice and dying.

It was a revolution born out of a real revolution, yet so tragically choked by a persistent void, its soul dripping with pontifications on egg quality. A void echoed, wrapped in silence, of egg pranksters imitating The March On Washington, crawling in the shadows of the Treason Trial, dwarfed by the valour of Tiananmen Square. There was a void, silence, because the revolution lacked its own breath, its own flame, because it insisted on saying the already said. It was stillborn, scorched by its avowal to creature comforts: air-conditioned meeting rooms, meeting schedules circulated weeks in advance, expensive perfumes paid for by parents slaving in Johannesburg banks, in Pretoria homes, as drivers of midnight trains to ports, somewhere at the mouth of Cape Town and Durban seas. It was silent because it was scheduled, tame – while revolutions are supposed to be immediate, unpredictable and dangerous things. Yet it was not, not in the true sense of dangerous things, meant to forcefully alter things. It was a revolution concerning the quality of cafeteria eggs.

The revolutionary song was unflattering: 'De Bruine, De Bruine, rotten eggs De Bruine/ Did you lay, or buy/ These damned powdered eggs, De Bruine!/ Why, Oh why/ Wretched man De Bruine.' Dining-hall pot plants were watered with tomato sauce, cutlery bent, restrooms vandalised. Mr De Bruine, the acting dining-hall manager, grew tired of the increasing hooliganism of the egg revolutionaries. He simply ordered good eggs, and the banging on dining room tables and the insulting song fizzled away – with it the Political Tribe's seven-hour meetings that resolved to spill tomato sauce into plants. It was only weeks later that the revolutionaries realised just how personally De Bruine had taken the song. The already suspect cheese suddenly tasted like bath soap. The Tribe established an impromptu Cheese Committee to investigate, to report on the sudden drop in cheese standards.

But De Bruine also filled them with dread. Nothing escaped that owl with grey shoes, the balding goat walking around with his asthma spray. His pointed and ashy elbows. His hairy chest. His cheap socks and properly tied shoelaces. That squint eye behind gold-framed bifocal lenses, dangling from the sun-burnt rubbery neck with a beaded string. His chipped tooth, his undecided potbelly, his stumpy index fingers that searched for clauses in the University Constitution. As deputy head of the university's Disciplinary Committee, John de Bruine wielded considerable influence. He was a loner, upright, steely, not easily swayed by praise or loathing.

So when the Cheese Committee invaded his office, an already irritable De Bruine was furious: 'This is a place of learning! Not a five-star hotel! We do not offer gourmet tropical-island dishes here, never have, never will! It is either the eggs or the cheese. You cannot have both!' He swung from his office chair, a VHS tape in hand, jammed it into a video machine. It was footage from the dining-hall security cameras; footage that stopped the newly elected Cheese Committee in their tracks. He charged: 'I am curious, itching, wondering what the DC is going to think of such blatant disregard of tomato sauce? These things have to be accounted for. Every cent!'

He had the upper hand and knew it, thwarting the cheese revolution before it could begin. I pitied the Political Tribe, concerned with the quality of eggs, presiding over Cheese Committees. They needed to be freed, be woken from the deceptions of freedom. Freed from freedom. To be told that real revolutions come once in a lifetime, that a whole generation would die off, before anything resembling a worthy revolution comes along, that what follows such revolutions – the once-in-a-generation kind – were but ramblings of history, reminders of the greatness of the human spirit. They needed to starve, the lot of them, until they learned they were not revolutionaries – but rather interpreters of the revolution. All they did, big and small, was but a fleeting salute at real suffering, suffering that birthed freedom written in blood, caked menstrual puddles in detention, blood from steel-pipe floggings, face bashings against walls. Why, oh why, did the Political Tribe think eggs mattered in the realm of existence? An email interrupted my reflections on these matters . . .

From: RustyBell@campus.ac.za
To: Michael@campus.ac.za
Subject: Are You Serious?

Helo You,
I don't know whether to laugh or cry. To think that I have paraded my deepest thoughts and aspirations, fooled myself into thinking you were capable of loving me is beyond me. I am deeply ashamed and enraged that you knew this all along, yet accepted to almost be intimate with me. I admit I was maybe too pushy, too ahead of myself with the love stuff. But let's talk about it. How's your starving yourself and these deepest reflections you talk about going to help you become a normal, functional, even useful human being? Other clever people have families, confidants, people who love them.

What makes you think you're so much better and greater than everybody else? Of what use is a great mind if it becomes a prison, a disease, a curse, a profound gift that nobody knows of or cares about? I can make that happen, if you let me. Graduation is a year away. Question is, are you going to continue starving yourself, when this nation desperately needs thinkers, even of the starving kind? All I need from you is some commitment. That's all. Commitment that we will

be together, that you will forget about this Palesa ex of yours and her circus charades. Do you really want a clown for a wife, someone who befriends monkeys and camels for a living? There are, surely, more interesting people in the world.
That's all.
Love,
Rusty B.

* * *

From: Michael@campus.ac.za
To: RustyBell@campus.ac.za
Subject: I am Serious

Rusty,
Great discoveries are often born out of catastrophic confusions. One small correction: my life and thoughts are not limited to self-starvation. I have no comments about all other matters you raise, except to say I will, to preserve clarity of thought and feeling, not be responding to any emails or phone calls of any kind, until such time that I have made compelling sense of some rather personal and therefore private quests. These might take a lifetime.
Brotherly,
Michael

* * *

I spent seven days in Room 306, David Webster Hall, surviving on a jug of water, observing it cooling and heating to the whims of Johannesburg weather, expressing boredom the only way water knows how: with those undecided bubbles. It was only when hunger ceased to be a craving, a sensation, that the world blurred into streaks of white light, that sounds seemed faint and distant. I at times feared I was losing my mind, worried I had pushed too hard into the unknown.

The world seemed to be swarming with insects, tiny silverish things hovering in mid-air, threatening to steal all the oxygen, leaving me weak and breathless. Palesa – whom I shall tell you more about – understood my predicament and, with feather-light cautions, encouraged my fifteen-day fasts. I asked if she thought I was losing my mind.

'No, Michael,' she said. 'You're just hungry. Bodies are designed to want food.' I smiled meekly. 'We have a new elephant,' she reported. 'I named her Moxie. It doesn't have any special meaning or anything, just seemed to me an elephant-like, playful, graceful, circus-like kind of name. Moxie. It has a ring to it, don't you think, a ring of a dependable friend?' I nodded. She was suddenly passionate, reflective: 'She's a beautiful animal. Calm-spirited. Wise. I have a feeling she knows things we will never fathom. That trunk. Hovering over things. Silently sniffing. What do you think? D'you think Moxie is a cute name?' I smiled, said I needed to rest. Palesa pressed my palm, like one bids farewell to a comatose, dying patient. 'I will leave these grapes and yoghurt here,' she said, 'in case you decide to nibble something.' I nodded. I supposed she went back to work, to the Johannesburg Zoo, but I didn't ask. I must have dosed off.

The fast was draining. First there were the fading hunger pangs, a microscopic throbbing of the bone marrow, a plunge into what seemed like warm fog. It was in the depths of that world, which was like walking through angry clouds, that I was besieged by the most colourful of dreams: children playing with hoola hoops on sand dunes, donkeys roaming free through expansive vineyards, that jacaranda-lined dirt road that led to my school, its gardens adorned with purple flowers and buzzing bees. I was, in my mind's eye, that eight-year-old who ran carefree around school grounds, my eyes fixed on a kite fluttering above, once again that twig-legged rascal who dreaded thunder claps, whose nose remembered each teacher's perfume, the dash of onion that lingered in their breath as they pressed their cheeks to mine, knowingly saving me from the horrors of mathematics.

I once again heard Teacher Moleleki, the crucifix of her rosary hovering inches above my sums, say: 'Four minus two equals two. Minus means we are taking away. Taking two away from four leaves us with two, because two twos make four.' Her patience was partly her knowing, her refusal to accept that I hated mathematics, that I found it pointless. An unwelcome strain on the mind. I was, in my starvation, once again in that revered choir, marching with Gestapo precision, around the school block, singing: 'Bajuda ba bolaile Jesu/ Bajuda ba bolaile Jesu/ Ba mmapola sefapanong/ Ba mmapola sefapanong/ Taba ye ke taba e bohloko/ Ba mmapola sefapanong.'

I wept every time we sang it, every time I pictured the horrors depicted in its lyrics. It amazed me that I still awoke, fifteen-odd years later, heartsore at the memory of our Gestapo-like choral passions. Dr West's face lit up at the discovery of this detail and, after two hours of probing yet open-ended questions, said he understood why the Jews killing Jesus and nailing him to a cross would, given Jesus' admirable virtues, be traumatic to a child, confirmed by the song's resolution: that the killing was painful news indeed.

So it was that Dr West added 'over-sensitivity' to my diagnosis, cautioning: 'Some people are a touch too tender-hearted, Michael. It is not an ailment, not in the medical sense, but a gift of sorts. Problem is, the world is indifferent to such people.'

I drifted in and out of dream states – completely lost track of time, of the world and its murderous Jews, of the distant rumble of thunder, a rumble that hinted that something great and unknowable lurked in the universe. I drifted back to small discoveries: tyrant winds that could blow birds' nests from the long limbs of jacaranda trees, leaving shivering pink chicks helpless in advancing dust storms; the effortless pleasure of sharpening a pencil, how the pencil peel folded itself into a miniature flower impression; how inky pens ruined shirt pockets; how army ants terrorised sickly praying mantises; the subtle crack of sand granules under soles of our polished shoes. It was during those dreamy states that a cat visited me, unhinged such an elaborate tale that left me perspiring, gasping for breath. It frustrated me a great deal so that neither Rusty Bell nor Dr West believed me when I told them of the visit from the cat. Dr West laughed, shrugged it off as some unlikely piece of information. But I know what I saw and, though Dr West dismissed me as 'going through mental difficulties', I have no doubt in my mind that, yes, generally speaking, cats cannot speak, but equally that this particular one was something quite different. An arrogant cat, I must add: thoughtful, brisk in temperament and, such a gifted teller of tales.

It was after my criss-crossing visions that I, very faintly, heard my dorm door open, someone walk in. It closed with a hesitant click. I, though half conscious, sensed a presence. The intruder slid in beside me, caressed my forehead with an open palm. I could tell, from the long fingers and mint hand cream, that it was Rusty. Palesa's hands were on the warm side, considerate in their touching and grabbing of things. A tongue moistened my ear lobes, slithered its way to my shut eyes, before embalming my dry, scaly lips. There was at once heavy breathing, as that tongue left a moist track along my forehead, as those long fingers helped themselves to the only organ morally and philosophically supposed to be mine – until I felt sudden exposure, those intrusive fingers fishing my firming organ from its slumber, positioning it for entry. The siege did not end until my asset collided with the coarseness of hair, a moist orifice, the contracting squeeze of a famished cunt, as she mounted me like a jockey; said I was the loveliest creature alive.

I was too weak to answer, too hungry to even open my eyes. She, even with my tears rolling down my temples, continued her assault, all the while moaning, whimpering: 'Forgive me, Michael. Forgive me.' I must have drifted out of consciousness then, for I woke up lost, with a lingering soreness, distant pain pricking my defenceless rod. I thought, so this is how it feels. To be defiled. There was, even in my dream state, my weakened hibernation, punctuated only by Palesa bringing custard, demands of the bladder, the odd shower, a furious rage, a fragility of spirit against my assault. It wounded me greatly knowing that Rusty Bell held keys to my secret bunkers – that there was, even there, in my ocean-deep escapes, the possibility of brutes on the lookout for weakness, on a mission to steal passions denied them by starving idealists, to wreck others in the name of love.

I was again plunged into toddler-like sleep, my rage blunted by memories of childhood sympathies: pity felt for the one-eyed boy named Moses (mercilessly teased), heartache for half-hatched chicks blown from nests ravaged by devilish winds, a knotted throat for a horse mercilessly lashed for visibly and not unreasonably being tired (blazing sun, tonnage fit for eight-wheeler trucks), clenched teeth for my then desk mate Palesa, who survived torrents of epileptic fits. But there were light-hearted moments, good memories, too: a breeze whistling through Alexandra Primary's rose bushes, love-struck pigeons cooing bird affections, jacarandas drizzling their purple magic on school grounds. I woke momentarily, sipped water, before submitting to the refuge of my meditative sleep.

* * *

I was, because of my excavations of the mind, not conclusively sure if Rusty Bell had indeed defiled me. I could have imagined it, hallucinated. Yet my soul confirmed otherwise – that something dreadfully sinister had taken place. It was in the way I remembered vague details, the long fingers locating and grabbing things with impunity, that I knew there were compelling grounds to break the fast – to return to the world, as most know it. Besides, my excavations unearthed all sorts of assaults on sanity, and it was only a matter of time before there would be a drift into the unknown. The body revolted against food, the mind against false logic of egg revolutions, the heart against Rusty's love snares.

Palesa told of charming incidents of her deepening friendship with Moxie, away from circus throngs, private moments of munching oranges and trunk rubbing, gentle murmurs and tusk holding. The weeks that followed were vague and purposeless, detached, in that I had – in my starvation – learned a sobering truth: that the mind, like sex, is too great, too deep an ocean to be known: its sandy confusions, the vivid coral reefs of its entombed yearnings, shark nests of nightmares past, the swirling waves of its power, mercilessly out of step with the blind faith of the heart. A certain clarity emerged, excavating elaborate but unrecognisable treasure troves from the seabed, a discovery that said: for all its expansive tricks, life remains sand-granule-sized portions of existence. Sobering. Sacred almost. Worthy of starvation.

This, I reasoned with myself, was not some lame discovery arrived at when choking on McDonald's burgers or dabbling in matrimonial equations, but a cold stare at the near-worthless sum total of all human knowledge. The universe laughs at humans, Masters of Creation, battling to understand the purity of things: the crystal perfection of a hailstone, the momentary glow of distant lightning from behind clouds, the distinct scent of a newborn baby. An email, however, sent shockwaves through my new-found life equations:

* * *

RUSTY BELL

From: RustyBell@campus.ac.za
To: Michael@campus.ac.za
Subject: Good and Bad Things Happen

Helo Michael,
I know you probably never want to ever see me again – something I totally accept and understand. But, but – though clearly wrong and shameful – I did what I thought to be the best for our future. Please accept my deep-set regret and apology for sneaking up on you like that – practically almost committing a crime. But there is some good news: what a treat! You are as manly as I had imagined, only a thousand times better.
Yours,
Rusty B.

* * *

I was, four months later, still dazed and appalled by the matter-of-fact confirmation of my rape when Abednego rang me to say Rusty had left campus (without saying a word) to be in her mother's care in Eldorado Park. She had taken ill and had been rushed to hospital. Tense and instructive, Abednego said he expected me to take responsibility for my actions. Or else.

I took exception to this veiled threat – told him point blank that I was, if anything, considering going to the police. I was, to the best of my knowledge, not a father to anyone, and therefore not expected to sprint to hospital wards at a moment's notice. Days crawled by, with me surviving on custard and jelly, the occasional fruit, steamed vegetables. But bodies are not designed for custard; custards are there to fool bodies and taste buds, not to truly sustain a life. The fast made lectures torture: vague, hazy, long-winded. It was Dr West's medical note (mental strain, recommended bed rest) that bought my freedom, the privilege of receiving lecture notes and reading lists to ponder and absorb in my own time. Rusty's veiled confession weighed on me, demanded increased solitude. Another eight weeks, blurry and detached, snailed oppressively past, my life dreamy, sleep patterns erratic.

* * *

At the Braamfontein police station a sleepy mood lingered – sleep owed to uniformed bodies dozing to crackling sounds of two-way radios, announcing capture of fugitives, some Alpha-Charlie-Tango gibberish. Nothing spectacular to note, just normal police-station scenes: a lone soul in handcuffs, the thud of stamps on a myriad statements under oath. It then dawned on me, as I exchanged greetings with a policeman sipping coffee from a mug designed for the greedy, that I was about to set a criminal trial in motion. She handed me those official papers, to set down my grievance, her pink and red and blue stamps at the ready, to ignite a chain reaction sure to end with Rusty Bell caged in some facility somewhere.

Yet I was hesitant. The longer I stood in front of the police officer, pen in hand, she looking blankly at me, the more I felt drained, suspicious of the avenues that lead to justice. The wall clock struck 3 p.m., and I – at exactly 3.15 – changed my mind, and decided to let it all go. Still wounded. Still raw. Still offended.

I handed Officer Ntuli her pen and statement, with only the date and two incomplete sentences: '3 September, two thousand and whatever. My name is Michael, a third-year student at the University of the Witwatersrand. I was in day eleven of my fast when Ms Rusty Bell, a close friend of mine . . ' All that scrutiny. The cross-examinations. Review of the facts. Review of review of the facts. Adjournments. The unfair, intrusive prosecutor's questions. Was it the first time you and the defendant were intimate? What would you say was your state of mind at the time of the alleged rape? Are you telling this court that you starved yourself for several days – that you cannot tell if it was in fact a rape or consensual – except the single email from the defendant? Should this court prosecute Ms Bell because she has conscience, because she is remorseful? You, in your email here, speak of quests that might take a lifetime. Kindly enlighten this court as to what those quests might be. Is it correct that you are undergoing therapy, that is: multiple consultations with a psychiatrist? For what reason, exactly? Would it be unfair to conclude that you are mentally under strain, depressed even and, therefore, not in a position to make such an accusation, with far-reaching implications? You have, on more than three occasions, checked Ms Bell's breasts for cancer lumps – an intimate act of trust and caring, I must add, because that was the nature of your relationship! Doesn't it follow, therefore, that it was not completely unreasonable for the defendant to expect intimacy from yourself?

Why shouldn't this court conclude that all your submissions are malicious – noting that you are in fact happily seeing or used to see another woman, a certain Palesa, I believe? You are, by all indications, a wise young man. I have no stomach for philosophy myself – but judging by the content and insight of your notes on the margins of these books, it is not every day or a coincidence that Pascal and Nietzsche are given such painstaking reading and reflection.

Enlighten this court, if you will, why the selective and self-serving acts of starvation and celibacy? I put it to you: the reckless manner with which you make this grave accusation is not consistent with your IQ. Why should this court waste valuable time pursuing petty ego trips? What are you not telling this court?

The assault, of course, would continue – with worse intrusions, designed to engender doubt and non-existent probabilities. All I knew, all I wanted to conclude and say, was that Rusty had wronged me. That is all. It was peculiar how time suddenly flew past, before I could make sense of my life, make sense of the loose ends that were supposed to reflect me to me, as a complete being, not fragments, at the mercy of would-be wives and prosecutors.

* * *

The second-floor wards at the Milpark Hospital were, except for a few unfortunate patients, deserted. Where had all the sick people gone? All the people with ruptured appendixes, with prostate issues, those thrown off motorbikes, others at the mercy of gastric whirlwinds, souls tormented by low blood pressures and renal failures, bleak tales of ovarian growths, of bone fractures, butchering of various kinds, lifelong tobacco abuse finally collapsing lungs, hearts skipping beats, their arteries clogged by fat and blood clots, neurological tremors, as well as inferno survivors mummified in bandages, zoo keepers mauled by lions, cases of vindictive malignant tumours – all reminders of human mortality, fragility?

A sign that read 'Maternity Ward' pointed towards elevators at the end of a long corridor. Once inside the elevator, I held its doors open for three nurses pushing a yelling old man. The man, a Mr Faizal, was apparently sick and tired of having latex-gloved hands explore him and, in his own words, was 'outraged by the indignities of fucking morphine'. Why couldn't he be left alone to die? he protested.

I overheard, as I exited the elevator, one of the nurses – the Indian one with bushy eyebrows – say I looked like I had seen a ghost. I followed the wall signs that led through automated glass doors, into a world of innocence: newborns in the throes of sleep, temperamental ones yelping, beaming mothers and grateful fathers in tight hugs. Babies held against bosoms turgid with human milk, babies yawning in solitary cots, babies vomiting on well-wishers, babies swarmed by beaming next of kin, a baby sucking a thumb, boy babies getting acquainted with breasts and nipples, things they would desire and chase over lifetimes, bottoms being cleaned, babies nestled in incubators.

The ward had a newness to it, a purity of sorts, an otherworldly pulse. It was a world charmed by the scent of baby shampoo, powders to welcome those toothless new *arrivants* from a multitude of wombs. Art on the walls was equally innocent: rabbits cuddling, sleeping lambs, fire engines exclaiming *beep beep*. It was a beautiful world, a world of regulated noise, an existence brimming with palpable bliss, bliss that seemed to radiate from creatures that knew nothing about anything, so blissfully and temporarily shielded from the barbed wires of adult worlds. The new *arrivants*, with their clear consciences, beaming beings without the slightest of secrets, without wants and yearnings, lovers or foes, without as much as something as worthless as boredom. It was with these reflections that a Matron Khumalo, grey-haired and full-figured, fatigued yet pleasant, asked whom I had come to see.

'Baby Michael, I believe,' I said.

'You the father?' she asked, adjusting her epaulettes.

'Technically speaking, yes. Morally and philosophically, no. But it is a very long story.'

A cloud descended over her radiant face. She cleared her throat, placed a professional and motherly hand on my shoulder. 'Your lovely girlfriend is stationed at Bed 8C, next to Baby Benton at that corner. She's undergoing tests on the fifth floor. But her mom and dad are with Michael Junior. Come with me,' she added, the motherly hand rubbing and squeezing my shoulder. I was unprepared for the paediatric ICU – but it had nothing to do with Abednego weeping over the longest prayer I ever heard, complete with the trials and tribulations of the children of Israel, how even pharaohs were no match for the Righteous Might of the Lord.

What I saw weakened my knees, snapped every nerve end of feeling. So, I concluded, this is the result of Rusty's long-fingered *coup d'état*, her ambivalent robbery of a Michael who lay starving, a crime unlikely to ever be understood, prosecuted, punished to the furthest and yet most appropriate sanctions justice permitted. The wall inscriptions, signs pointing out directions to the maternity and other wards, reminded me of arrows drawn on the wall tiles of campus toilets, arrows that drew attention to specific jottings amid a web of insults and poetic fumbling, a battle for prominence between graffiti and selected wall vandalisms (someone had rubbed a coin, defaced the white tiles until they turned a rusty green), amid lewd drawings and confirmations of loneliness (please call Maxwell on 088 773 4344 anytime), general outbursts without provocation or purpose.

Three particular inscriptions stood out: the 'Don't sit and wonder, shit like thunder' note inscribed with a red marking pen in cubicle 3 of the Senate House restrooms, the 'I came looking for knowledge, but found pussy instead' in cubicle 4 of the Africana Library toilets, under which an anonymous poet was inspired to record: stop it already/ this bullshit about nation/ about negation of alienations/ impressions calculations estimations /fragments of nation/ draped in mysteries of what ifs/ colourless/ like water. Such impatience. Such bleak resignation of a fledgling poetic talent.

A CAT NAMED CLINTON K

I cannot help that the world is swarming with sceptics. Dr West, for one, never believed me, which is a shame to his profession. But I know what I saw. I swear on my life that a cat visited me during my eleven-day fasts. Clinton, as far as I understand him, was a prankster and crude show-off, polished only in his hogging of the limelight. He not only gave animals a voice – something even I, in my ramblings, had never given a second thought before our encounter – but was also both entertaining and serious. Perhaps, in a way, I saw Clinton as my complement . . . Were we both not cerebral in our views. What I know for sure, however, is that we were not diametrically opposed, Clinton and I. He sat on the windowsill of my David Webster dorm room, next to my jug of water, and addressed me thus:

'Allow me to introduce myself: my name is Bruno. That is what I am expected to answer to, these days. I have been called many things before, depending on the household and the imagination of its inhabitants. I was Julius Caesar once (how charming), when I belonged to the Smiths in Somerset West, Booby (erotic, I tell you!) when I pranced around the Zulu home in Port Elizabeth, Neptune to an aged plumber in Soweto. I was Butch to a Johannesburg vet who saved me from a lung infection (you're not completely useless, humans) and, Tyson to the Buthelezis, despite my revulsion and utter disdain for sweaty half-dressed men punching each other for money.

'There was that not-so-bright Professor Newton, who named me Knock Kness – KK for short – a human defect, or maybe out of pure laziness, I could never tell. I came very close, as close as close shaves go when it comes to yonder worlds. It's a miracle that I, a cat, am here, talking to you, for in reality, I should long be dead. I don't have to mention that a human had something to do with my near demise. Big Bruce, the veteran pimp at Purple Moon, a seedy nightclub downtown, shot at me – all six bullets and missed. You would think I'd committed treason. When asked, Big Bruce – his thick, meaty and sweaty neck draped in necklaces thick as chains on construction sites, his eyes bloodshot, his gold-plated front tooth hinting at a predisposition for chaos – simply hissed: "Because I can."

'Paloma, a sadistic young devil, raised amid drunks and talented pole dancers, had been brutalising me with a plastic sword for months – between which she relished twisting my tail, laughing heartily when I writhed in pain. Bruce urged her on, showered her with praise. "That's my little pirate," he grinned. "Tough as nails." His Little Pirate burnt me with molten candle wax, sent her shoes (oh, the terror of that giant buckle on one of her particularly solid pair of winter boots) flying towards me like scud missiles under tables, behind couches, and from under bar stools where I had run for my life. There was a broken broomstick, with which she was particularly vicious. I limped for seventeen solid days following that assault, which was, like the others, unprovoked. It rained blows – with anything Paloma could lay her hands on: ashtrays, wine bottles, leftover T-bones from patrons' dinner plates. Yet I remained calm, even though seething inside, so enraged and on the edge that I could have killed that Little Lucifer.'

Someone flushed a toilet somewhere in the direction of the television room.

'Since when is being born a cat such an unforgivable crime?' continued the cat. 'Why did such abuse continue unabated? With lukewarm, half-hearted, absent-minded and matter-of-fact admonishing of that sadistic little tyrant who reigned supreme? She was Bruce's daughter, you know. Legend has it that this was a man who seldom slept. His drug-fuelled anger was legendary, earned him a reputation, and unless suicidal, no one dared to, as he cautioned, "push his buttons". It was this mean streak that was also evident in his Little Pirate, that chubby little devil, whose cruelty was beyond malice.

'What was a cat to do? What hurt me the most is that it never occurred to Bruce or his sordid clients that what that depraved little child thought amusing was not in the least funny – me having to always look over my shoulder for variations of pain that seemed to stretch to eternity.

'Aren't cats also flesh and blood? Two years of that torment drove me to the unthinkable, when following an evening of unprecedented torture, I finally – not without great difficulty, I have to say – decided to teach the little Lucifer a lesson, so brutal that it left the repugnant little horror one-eyed. A swift strike with determined claws, then gasps from Purple Moon patrons and a bloody eyeball drove Bruce into a murderous rage, resulting in those gunshots, which by the grace of I-don't-know-what – all missed, of course.'

A butterfly, small and insignificant, missed perching onto my water jug and plunged into my drinking water; an accident Clinton K observed with a sense of detachment, plunging back into his story: 'I met little Paloma at Purple Moon,' continued the cat, 'uninvited, scavenging for food. That pest's abuse of me will go down in history as the greatest injustice against an esteemed member of the cat family, bringing back – as it did – unpleasant terrors lurking in the shallow graves of memory. I must stress that I was, before I found myself at Purple Moon, never in the habit of hanging around whorehouses. It happened quite by accident, a shameful development, following me running away from home. It was not really running away – I simply got tired of being a pet to one Marcus Broderick: a useless, talentless, would-be poet who never published a single stanza.

'A bachelor, never married, a face choking under facial weed, the bony poet almost starved me to death with his lack of ambition. The skeletal Mr Broderick lived on a diet of bananas, expecting me to hustle for my own food. I hated him, sometimes pitied him, how he dragged his bony frame around that average house: not plush, somewhat promising, generally depressing. It wasn't a house, really, but a three-bedroomed flat at Casablanca Heights in Hillbrow. I could not stand his mumbling into the phone, battling to convince editors and publishers that there was, in fact, literary merit to his poems. Failing, he slammed the phone – smashed anything within reach against the walls: notebooks, coffee mugs, a photograph of his brother.

'I found this throwing of objects traumatic. I got fed up with Marcus mumbling into the phone, his temper tantrums, his wanting to own a pet when he couldn't even afford tea bags (a single tea bag recycled, expected to miraculously yield twenty cups?) . . . Shameful, if you ask me. I did not even bother saying goodbye, more so because Marcus had a lady friend visiting, an occurrence that happened once in a blue moon: that Thelma with facial moles and mauve skirts. Marcus conveniently forgot that cats are prone to hunger and thirst. On those hideous green couches they sat, he and Thelma, looking into each other's eyes, transfixed, awkward, unlikely romantic figurines.

'So I left, raided dustbins for anything edible, threw up at the filth that human generate: bloody rags, rotting meat crawling with maggots, rubbery and oily bag-like things dripping with mucus-like secretions – the true identity of which I learned years later: birth-control tools humans use to shield themselves from unwanted births and embarrassing ailments – an odd chicken wing here, a half-eaten grilled fish there, some meatballs under orange peels and, on a good day, some KFC remains.'

I cast my eyes on a stack of books that adorned my study table: musings on divorce, mortality, and Aristotle. The cat paused, and then continued.

'There were new tragedies to deal with. Stray dogs suddenly leaped out of nowhere, fangs bared, spoiling for a fight. Dreadful Johannesburg thunderstorms and motorists whose driving antics seemed a single-minded crusade to run over cats. It was during one of those chilly downpours, with explosive thunder claps, that I fell down a manhole (why was that gaping hole left to swallow me whole?), tossed and sucked by a whirlwind of raging storm drainage water, the closest I have ever come to drowning. I held on for dear life, my claws sunk into some rusty and rapidly perishing steel pipe, wide-eyed at the possibility that that was to be my last day on earth. It was my desperate miaows that caught a passerby's attention.

'Who would have thought that humans are capable of hearing, of summoning a rescue team: fire engine, dive swimmers, blinding searchlights to save handsome me, a cat, from what seemed like certain death? They spoke of hypothermia, dehydration and trauma, before imprisoning me in a mobile penitentiary, whisking me to some animal care centre named Noah's Ark. It was at that centre, on a cushioned prison cell, with annoying hounds for neighbours barking their heads off, that I drifted into terse sleep.

'The food was good (but nothing to rave about), the head veterinarian had foul garlic breath, and the obviously lazy cleaners reluctantly cleaned away dog droppings and urine that assaulted my nostrils. None of them seemed clever at all – so I kept to myself, for I despise shallow conversations, useless navel gazing. Rabbits. Parrots. Pythons. Owls. Other cats. A tortoise. Hamsters. Of course humans came to adopt a pet or two, their little terrors for children in tow, chubby little fingers browsing our caged enclosures for an animal friend, something to rule and preside over, something to brutalise.

'It was a hopeless time, unworthy of the grand plan of my life. I was, by week three – even given my general wariness of human beings – begging for human companionship: all that barking, that chirping, that horrid-looking tortoise estimated to be 73, the occasional mouse (how I trembled, fearing a bubonic plague outbreak) that ventured past our temporary prisons in search of food and warmth. Three more weeks and still not a soul granted me a second glance, something that would have happened (some human, taking interest in me), had it not been for those seedy, over-enthusiastic, uncouth dogs.

'I found their whines, their melodrama, their wagging of tails nauseating to say the least – all that yelping and prancing about, tongues dripping with unmentionables, the inferior beasts. I must admit that being ignored wounded my ego, forced me to almost submit to the grand lie that humans are masters of earthly existence. New dogs came. Human fingers pointed, and chose. I wallowed in despair, retreated to the furthest corner of my kennel, played dead. No one seemed to care: there were simply too many admissions, too many mouths to feed, and those attention-seeking hounds to compete with.'

The butterfly finally gave up trying to escape the water jug, submitted to death by drowning. The cat was unmoved, and continued as if nothing had happened.

'Which brings me back to Paloma. I've been rather harsh, I know, but in truth, in my deepest of bosoms – the broomstick assaults not considered – I had great love and admiration for that girl child: her lovely moonlike eyes, those chubby cheeks, and that sculptured little mouth worked itself into scornful twitches as she rained broomstick blows on me. Watching her sleeping was humbling; how innocent and harmless she became as her sleepy nostrils twitched to a bothersome housefly, as she stretched her torso (wrapped in pink pyjamas, with red elephant artwork) to sleep-induced numbness, the magnetic pleasure of watching that tiny mouth yawning and the little body tossing, settling into an invisible sleep cocoon, those sadistic paws away from the broomstick.

'I loved her because she was so lovable, adored her, for what else is one supposed to do with children but love them? I do think, in hindsight, that I might have perhaps, just a little, overplayed my hand in scratching her eye out. But wasn't my anger, my fury, completely within reason, every living thing's God-given right to defend itself, against an innocent child in the company of grown men and women, even if they were more concerned with swinging their bare buttocks in the faces of awestruck admirers, oblivious to the broomstick blows that ultimately pushed me beyond limits, resulting in a marble-eyed Paloma, who will for the duration of her life be reminded: never piss off cats.

* * *

'I spent sixteen weeks in captivity at Noah's Ark. There is no shred of doubt in my mind that I was mildly depressed, exhausted, and generally suicidal. My life had been, at least up until my confinement at that animal shelter, largely lonely and unremarkable. For someone of my intellect, my inbred humour in the face of breathtaking stupidity leaking from so-called pet lovers – sordid and depraved creatures not entitled or qualified, not even in the remotest of possibilities, to own and preside over a cat's life, let alone a polished specimen of my calibre – allowed me brief moments of comic relief.

'To be brought into a household, under the pretext of hunting and murdering rats, is to me the greatest insult ever to be cast on dynasty after dynasty of self-respecting cats, who – unaware of this abuse – go so far as to risk their lives killing pit vipers, which as it was evident from one or two isolated and unfortunate incidents, had no intention of showing them mercy. Death by puff adder venom. In your limited thinking and, dare I say dim conclusions, you humans have somehow concluded that the horrors of the world, including snake bites and the tortures of bubonic plagues, is something cats do not reflect about, hold any opinions on. So the world has rat populations, greasy eyesores the size of rabbits breeding under Johannesburg's sewers: but why is this a problem of cats?

'Why was I, at Purple Moon, expected to simply pounce on and murder rats without provocation – complete strangers? For the love of pets, I hear you say. Love? What love, of a cat, rests on the expectation that cats should always murder rats? Not that I am sorry that dogs are expected to bark at strangers, provide false security to helpless humans by baring fangs at would-be intruders. Far from it. My revolt is based on principle: the view that – as far as I can see, established human expectations notwithstanding – I will never blunt by claws pouncing on mice, creatures that by their very design thrive in filth!' The butterfly had in its struggle, its denial of death, of drowning, sheared a wing off, a wing that now floated independently in the water jug.

'Likewise,' continued Clinton K, 'I will never, to the amusement of observing humans, risk my life or waste cat acrobatics killing snakes, in whose intended destinations and life stories I haven't the faintest interest. I, therefore, refuse to be drawn into obscure and vague grudges between human and mouse, between human and snake. To that end, my intellect does not allow me to degrade myself, to – even with facts and superior reason starring me in the face – make a fool of myself amassing rat corpses for the rest of my days. There is, surely, or at least must be, more inspiring and stimulating aspects to life than murdering carriers of bubonic plague? That said, I am not against anyone objecting to my analysis, this momentous contradiction of children's love affairs with Mickey Mouse, and their parents' murderous instincts at the mere suspicion, a possibility, of Mickey in the flesh, cohabiting with them.

'You would have by now, if you are wise, deciphered that I am not of average intellect, Michael (that's the name on your student card), that my reflections about life and living are far greater than the mess humans have landed us animals in: animals in zoo cages the world over, experimental breeding with the most depressing and grotesque of results, and the great lengths humans go to breed animals for the sole and profane purpose of slaughter. Some of us, particularly domesticated cats of my ilk, witness humans at their most vulnerable, in their most despicable of states: following wives from room to room, trousers bulging, begging for knickers to be lowered, unleashing belt thrashings on otherwise innocent kids in the name of uprooting ill discipline (a lost pencil case), when the real frustration is the wife accusing the husband of having little or no ambition ("Your friends own beachfront homes", "Of all the world's sluts, you had to succumb to Molly Stevens of the facial moles?", "I dread the day when that balding will take full effect, Tom – your head already looks like a casket lid.")

'I have seen them, Michael, seen them all: noses dripping with mucus, in the throes of influenza; stuffing their offspring with pork chops – a recipe for premature heart disease; observed them butcher each other during jealous love skirmishes; fishing and sniffing panties of visiting relatives from laundry baskets; prancing about the house in the nude; men nursing skew potbellies and pencil-thick stretch marks; winces and bellows of pain from behind lavatory doors as piles dealt their anal blows; midnight sneaking and tiptoeing to balconies to appease cigarette and whisky addictions; the heart-wrenching disdain with which wives treat their mothers-in-law; the inconsolable sobs of mourners at the funerals of people they hated when alive; and humans generally being human: watching way too much television, groping each other in the presence of startled children.

'How can you possibly be the superior species, worthy of being custodians of God's grand plan, sitting at the apex of decency, for – as we often hear – humans are not animals, and therefore somehow entitled to the most perplexing of contradictions?'

The cat paused, raised a paw as if gesturing to stress a salient point and, continued:

'I am quite aware, Michael, that I risk this – my considered reflections on the greatest lie dwarfing creation, that humans are masters of creation – coming across as rants from an arrogant cat with certain justified mouse and snake phobias. The heart of the matter, in part, is this: no one, not even God, had the courtesy to understand the world from the point of view of cats, that is, domesticated cats that in many instances end up as part of the furniture in obscene households of frustrated poets dabbling in tantrums and intimacies with whores, that misguided Paloma child with her broomstick-wielding ways, or the indifference of care places with their animal orphans, man-made sewer pipes in which, were it not my appreciation of the gravity of life, I would have perished.

'It is possible and, I suppose not unreasonable, that you will think me a voice in the wilderness: callous sentiments are to be expected from human sympathisers – who, following centuries of brainwashing, cannot tell the difference between milk and good tea. I must hasten to add that I am a great lover of tea, and not – as is popular opinion – foamy liquids from udders of cows. Is that strange, that inconceivable, that a cat would be lactose intolerant? Why has it been assumed that all cats, millions and counting, somehow have a natural inclination to milk, an inferior drink in my opinion, that does nothing but brew bloated bowels? I learned of the beauty of tea, its majestic assault on the taste buds, from sucking on newly discarded tea bags in dustbins, weeks following my escape from Purple Moon, from Paloma, whose unprovoked broomstick blows would have eventually crippled me.

'It was in those dustbins, while I was on the run from Paloma and her father's bullets, from that untalented and depressed poet, that I experienced some of the appalling variety of foods that pass human plates and palates. This is, in itself, not a problem – except that we animals, cats included, are expected to risk oral hygiene murdering rats! Not that I promote the massacre of birds, but there is a certain grace, a nobility, in cats catching birds mid-air, for if truth be told – bearing in mind isolated cases of avian flu – birds are not too bad a meal for an adventurous cat. Besides, it can and should be argued that repeated, mid-air capture of birds is good exercise for cats, for though naturally agile, no self-respecting pussy wants to be fattened into a furry, bulky irritant that spends hours crouching on couches and under tables, with no zest for life. The nimbler the body, the sharper the mind.

'Put simply, I would not be sharing this tale, with its precisions, were it not for my good fortune, an incident that almost redeemed mankind, when a certain judge, whom I mistook for a bachelor, rescued me from the animal welfare centre. It was at his apartment, Apartment 1806, Maude Street, Sandton City, that I was introduced to the charms of scholarship, Constitutional Law, and a dash of International Relations. For a man with that amount of money, of such esteemed social and professional stature, Judge Peterson is amazingly solitary in nature, measured in temperament and studious to a fault.

'The apartment, on the eighteenth floor, presides over the Sandton cityscape, and offers the most spectacular views of traffic moving soundlessly along tree-lined streets by day and horizons of dazzling lights come evening. I must admit to it being intimidating, terrifying even, being so high up in the clouds, where Johannesburg thunderstorms brew unsettling clouds, explosive lightning strikes.

'A three-bedroomed apartment, 1806 is deceptively small on entry, but the space seemed to grow as I strolled past the exquisitely furnished reception and living areas, past the visitor room, that majestic kitchen that rivals the best on celebrity home television shows, the private study, and the master bedroom that boasts all sorts of heart-stopping charms – the most pronounced of which is the painted ceiling, depicting a little girl, basket in hand, running through an open field. The vastness of the space, of that girl running barefoot across the field, along a farm road towards a distant windmill, the road dotted with an odd lamb here, a guinea fowl there, almost moved me to tears each time the Judge, a small man eternally in three-piece suits, points at the running girl and says: "Life is not mysterious at all, Clinton. It's for free spirits."

'I cannot say I am not tickled by the great name the good scholar bestowed on me – for what cat, between here and the Strait of Gibraltar, as far as Budapest, Mongolia even, shares a name with the forty-second president of the United States? To make the distinction from and, I suspect, with respect to the former president, the Judge adds "Kitty" to my name. He addresses me as Clinton K in private, and abbreviates it to CK whenever we are in the company of others. I cannot say I have qualms about either variation of the name, for pompous as it may sound, I do, not without good reason, fancy myself capable of thinking reserved for distinguished heads of state.

'I swear I saw a lone tear drop into my companion's wine glass one afternoon – faintly heard him say, "Life. When are we ever gonna learn?" He brushed my back with an open palm, ever so gently, in slow jerky motions, and concluded: "Don't judge us too harshly, Clinton K. There are fools amongst us."'

I heard the wind rustle leaves strewn across the David Webster Hall parking area. I blinked, thirsty and delirious and, like that, Clinton K was gone.

FRANK & MARIA

I often found myself thinking a lot about my father. A Pretoria University Philosophy and Political Science dropout (second year), he always hoped to return to his studies, little knowing that bursaries could be temperamental – that they could dry up without forewarning. He could also not have planned that he would meet Maria, my bubbly mother, and that such a meeting would result in my conception three years later, a third attempt after two miscarriages. Studies in world political systems, Socrates and Kierkegaard stalled following my healthy and miraculous birth on 4 July, eyes open, via Caesarean methods, at a decisive weight of 3.8 kilograms.

I am reliably told, by both Frank and Maria, my parents, that no amount of bum smacking and considered pinching elicited the birth yelp from me, that I looked puzzled and a touch impatient. Mother objected to Frank naming me after Nietzsche, saying that that was too showy and un-African. I agree with Mother that, though somewhat catchy, with an intellectual ring of sorts, Nietzsche would have been an awkward name then and now. I, according to Mother, did not have a confirmed name for 96 days of my life, using Frank Junior, my father's name, as a placeholder name while debates and counter-proposals raged between Frank Senior and his Maria, proposals that included anything from famous mountain peaks in Africa to Egyptian pharaohs, narrowly missing famous inventors of the telephone and the bicycle in particular, skirting names of Christ's disciples by a hundred miles, touching on American Civil Rights leaders, before, on Day 96, Frank and his Maria agreed to go beyond the clouds, to an angel in heaven, thus naming me Michael.

Frank could have been a great banker, one of the greatest, if he hadn't been born at the wrong time and with the wrong skin colour. His acumen with money, his softest of hearts, did not earn him a cushioned life in the South Africa of then and of now. There was a measured pride about him, though, a discreet pride in how he chose to love a world that showered him with doubt and disdain. For as long as I can remember, my father worked as a delivery man for Almond & Spencer Pharmaceuticals, criss-crossing Johannesburg's avenues, responding to ailments of suburbia and, for extra income, weekend shifts transporting 'Urgent Medical Samples' for hospitals.

It was from this – what he called life's tragic pranks – that he managed to put me through school, that chinks appeared in his quiet pride, fissures that made his thoughts drift, prompting that heavy sigh and yearning: 'I would have loved to fly aeroplanes, Michael.' He later joined Harmony Gas & Fuels as a man who fought to be master of his life, but who instead helplessly watched as life and history drained all that was supposed to make life pleasurable, a drop at a time.

His was a life not lived, but leaked away, soundless, in the single-roomed tin shack we called home. There were very few certainties in my life, or any life for that matter, but there was never greater resolve than the fact that I deeply loved my father: his limp handshakes, his rare and brief laughter, his wise eyes, his long veranda reflections (newspaper in hand), how he would later, in silence, sit at our dinner table holding hands with 'the loveliest and most gifted seamstress in the universe' – my mother, a flame of a woman because of whom even priests momentarily had lapses of speech (My God, Maria, you married too quickly!) or action: how a visiting pastor from a neighbouring parish held on too long to Mother in what was supposed to be a cordial hug – a hug that ended with Pastor Immanuel's palms resting motionless on mother's hips. I wished father would reprimand such men, men with errant palms, but no, that seemed to add to his inner glow, his peculiar confidence.

As far as love goes – untainted, ocean-current love – none comes close to the one I witnessed in our one-room shack in Alexandra. It was not the kind depicted in lifestyle magazines: of walks along sunny boulevards, boat cruises on blue oceans, nose rubbing in restaurants. It was not, though it had a poetic glow, love spoken about by forlorn poets, not one of horse riding and romantic bicycle excursions into the countryside, not burdened by visits to the Eiffel Tower or the Taj Mahal. It was a love that had learned to ridicule lack, a brazen kind of feeling, resolute, daring even, so ahead of earthly imperfections that it seemed otherworldly: that silent hand holding of theirs, that drinking from one coffee mug when sugar was in short supply, the wrist rubbing and ear lobe nibbling (a fraction of a second this) on selected evenings, how Father never fixed his own cufflinks, never learned to master a tie, how Mother fixed those faultless tie knots, adjusting knot size and position, dealing with the odd, errant shirt collar, that open palm with which she ironed the tie onto father's chest, ending all her husband grooming with a kiss to the forehead.

Frank hurled an eighteen-wheeler truck across South Africa three weeks in the month, followed by four days of rest, most of which he spent either reading encyclopedias and aviation literature on the veranda or, looking into his Maria's eyes. There was nothing harmonious about Harmony Gas & Fuels: drivers died fiery deaths in collisions, the risk of arsonists' bullets aimed at puncturing petrol tankers in the hope of Hollywood-style explosions, the odd hijacking by petty fuel mafias.

It was timid work, reasonably tolerable, but far from harmonious. There were times when he transported only gas cylinders, which, when thought of scientifically, meant he was in the company of bombs by the truckload, a daunting and inescapable thought, entirely at the mercy of fate. Burning tankers made some of the news bulletins, black billowing smoke and sky-high flames: the sombre images of fire engines and ambulances. It was, on second thought, deadly work, lonely, almost suicidal, staring at the tarmac day and night, between Cape Town coastal refineries and Johannesburg inland garages, eyelids heavy as lead, fighting sleep.

For years he commanded the trucks, packed with gas cylinders and explosive liquids: through mountain passes, across vast grasslands, in crawling city traffic. It was unimaginative work, with nothing but the drone of the diesel engine for company, living on fatty takeaways, sleeping in desolate roadside motels. To my knowledge, Frank never harboured an interest in another plague that wiped out Harmony Gas

& Fuels' workforce over the years: roadside prostitutes. Even without him having said so, I from instinct knew that his love for his Maria far exceeded fondling against truck wheels, timed fucking in cheap hotels, on truck sleeper beds. There was, however, despite the potential of a fiery demise or driving into a bridge, perhaps great benefit in the routine and solitude of trucking – for I, without him saying so, wondered what open spaces could do to a mind.

What ponderous character did mile after mile of driving engender? What precision of thought comes with years of harrowing experiences: faulty brakes, tyre blowouts, gas leaks, engine failures, fever bouts and revolting bowels? He probably thought about these things when rocking on that chair, encyclopedia in hand, momentarily raising his eyes to ask: 'Did you know, Michael . . . Ahmed Baba was a great African scholar. Timbuktu. Astrology. Astronomy. Philosophy. He authored over one thousand manuscripts.' There were countless Did-You-Know questions, on subjects that struck him as worthy of knowledge. He always said, calmly and reflectively, that he would one day cease to drive trucks, noisy and unyielding things, and fly aeroplanes instead. This sentiment was oft repeated, without a deadline or concrete plan, the only measure of which was the thrifty way in which Frank lived, how he spent hours reading, anything and everything on aviation. The more I scrutinised Frank, the more I wondered if he was emotionally stable, if he could, as his dream job required, make countless split-second decisions.

According to wisdom posted on Google, air traffic controllers are required to have excellent situational awareness. Brilliant short-term memory. That would be a burden on Frank, who also had to be quick and assertive in his decision-making abilities, including performance under duress. Everything about managing airport goings-on demanded excellence of many kinds: numeric computations, focus on exact language (words) spoken from fifteen thousand feet above the ground, in aircraft cruising at mind-boggling speeds, exact words devoid of the potential for misunderstanding. Just how good would this truck driver be? And why was I so obsessed with putting him on the scale, brooding over so many things he left unsaid? If I asked him, as I have for many years, the answers remained the same: 'You worry too much, Michael.' Or, 'I will think about it,' or that perplexing answer, accompanied by a series of small nods: 'I see you are curious, that's very good.' And still no answers.

No one, except Mother, seemed to believe he would one day leave Harmony Gas & Fuels, accept their fake gold watch, make a five-minute speech over muffins and bad coffee, shake hands with a representative of the representative of Harmony Gas & Fuels Inc. Group Managing Director: Southern Africa, pose for pictures taken with a picnic-like camera, possibly finally openly flirt with the fleet manager or receptionist, feign deep gratitude at receiving atrocious gifts from colleagues (cheap pine picture frames whose glue melted before his very eyes, a wall clock with all the hallmarks of pawnshop embarrassments, a pictorial book recording the cockroach species of the Amazon Basin), listen to selected people he knew hated him speak passionately and eloquently about what a loss his departure was to Harmony Gas & Fuels, more handshakes with fellow truckers suddenly realising the full weight of their paralysis, their enslavement, their limited options, pats on the back by yet more truckers who didn't know what they did not know, wishes for a bright future by gossiping mechanics and morbid inventory clerks, matter-of-fact memories of truckers who perished in explosive infernos.

An accountant with stained teeth would remind him of R4.26c still owed on a R17 000 loan from 1985, the mumbled 'For He's a Jolly Good Fellow' sung tragically off key, the equally bland 'hip-hip hoorays' dripping with anxiety and petty jealousies. There was a sobering truth: even if the Group Managing Director did not delegate Mr Conrad Buthelezi who, owing to a Disneyland trip with family, further delegated a Mr Chamberlain, who came himself to thank my father, the ceremony would still have had false importance because for every Frank downing tools, there were millions others doing the same: truckers on icy Canadian routes, midwives throwing in the towel in Mongolia, army men being blown to shreds by bullets and mortar fire in Mosul.

Like all sorts of souls finally abandoning their yokes, their enslavement by the likes of Harmony Gas & Fuels, Father was not what you would call 'Important'. He remained invisible between the cracks of modern South Africa, as employee No. 908/F of the Harmony Gas & Fuels Energy Division, driver of Truck 804, his importance obliterated by the middle class. Frank's invisibility was because of the middle class, Misters Buthelezi and Chamberlain who frequented Disneyland, the middle class who populated the Johannesburg cityscape: crawled around its malls, its picnic spots, sped along its motorways in cherry-red Porsche 911s, dozed behind desks in office parks, infested sporting arenas; professionals with heads stewing with profit-and-loss statements, divorce arguments and counter-arguments, political conspiracies, their sleep patterns ravaged by forensic investigations, joints swollen and creaky from gout and arthritis, visits to former lovers curtailed by restraining orders, creatures recovering from boardroom skirmishes; gloomy funeral directors and jumpy polishers of diamonds, stalker telemarketers and insurance salespeople, obese chefs, part-time writer dentists, temperamental producers of television shows, investigative journalists with their whisky-drenched entourages, Class-A whores at the service of bankers and errant university professors, engineers hawk-eyed at construction sites, beauticians debating skin types, auditors suddenly discovering arithmetical errors that would sink corporations, professional fraudsters under house arrest, disgraced socialites bickering on aeroplanes. It was because of them that my father remained, largely, invisible.

What if this man, whom I so revered, had nothing to offer beyond sharing, in jumbled alphabetical order, contents of an encyclopedia? What if he was not wired for wisdom, not a creature of true pontification and reflection? Was it possible, or at least conceivable, that he had little to offer other than daydreaming on a rocking chair, tending carrot seedlings, pruning rose bushes? What if his languid silence, his faint nods, were admissions of failure, of emptiness, stupidity even? More disturbing was whether offspring could or should judge the cracks in the Franks of the world, the Franks who have willed them into existence? In a world of seven billion and counting, there surely were fathers who were less than bright, limited in their exploration of the world. Stupid. And even if that were true, proven by life's unforgiving yardsticks, voicing such in Africa, a continent in a world of dwindling cultures, was tantamount to exiling oneself in the eyes of many, who would without thinking say: 'He starved to death, to prove he was wiser than his own father, a man he branded a fool!' They would snub my wedding, my house-warming parties, some even my funeral, saying: 'Let him rise from those morgue refrigerators, dig his own damn grave if he's so wise.'

And in considering Frank, my father, I could not but help draw parallels between him and my Dr West, that other counsellor, air traffic controller on the runway that was to become my life. I was annoyed that Dr West refused to believe, to acknowledge, affirm the fact that a cat named Clinton K spoke to me. Clinton K, as I remember, put most psychiatrists to shame in his understated but incisive observation of the world. Why was Dr West, so practised in the avenues of the mind, its deceptions, known and unknown, so quick to deny, with a measure of certainty, that there could be, in this world blessed with trillions of cats, at least one capable of formulating arguments, enjoying being a prankster, telling tales? As much as I understood Dr West's professional responsibilities, which included guiding fervent minds from falling off cliffs, starvation in the name of spiritual transcendence, I found his detachment from the Clinton K episode disturbing to say the least, offensive even. I am certain, double sure, committed to the fact that a cat named Clinton K sat on my windowsill and, with admirable skill and exactitude, narrated terrors suffered at the hands of sadistic and inadequate humans. Clinton K, in his no-doubt cynical and devil-may-care arrogance, brought to the fore the reckless gallantry of humans, a recklessness entirely foreign to my own father, I am sure.

I was not sure what my father would make of my starvations, of the Clinton K episode, of Rusty Bell who prized and imagined tongues exploring *that* orifice, a corridor not intended for such. What would he make of Rusty Bell's long fingers, fingers that helped themselves to a tool philosophically meant to be mine, fingers that ultimately proved unwavering in the pilfering of life-giving seed, yanked from a hungry fantasist who lay in a daze, imagining the world as he would like it to be? Would the obligations of fatherhood oblige him to listen without judgement, offer alternatives – or would he, appalled by the content of my confessions – like Ms Bell of the honey-brown assets, Monica of the sculptured knees – be rattled, lost at sea, with rusty compasses? Just how unimportant was the former truck driver, dreaming of powerful authority to command the departure and arrival of aircraft from lookout towers? What did fifteen years of staring at the tarmac, inhaling diesel fumes, wrestling gas-cylinder tonnage, contribute to a man's knowledge, his sensibilities? What secret observations were offered by the many greetings and conversations exchanged with toothless shopkeepers in small, obscure towns? Was his supposed refusal to bed whores, a lack, a hurdle that chipped away at proper mastery of life's atypical musings: worlds of philosophical cats, egg revolutionaries, Kerushas with midnight calls announcing underwear phobias? What did this man, who had for a decade and half seen roads in all manner of variations: motorways covered in hailstones, some streaming with muddy rain water, others bloodied by carcasses of slain baboons, dusk and dawn cloud formations, the sweltering summer heat that reduced horizons to blurry, hazy conquests know? What did those lone hours, without the company of friend of foe, do to a man's mind, how he weighed his worth in the universe? Were they, the hours serenaded by the drone of the diesel engine, of any use in revealing a man to himself – nudging him, later strangling him, forcing him for fifteen years to drive the same tedious routes with practised submission, chronic boredom, measured indifference?

Did this explain why Frank's peers took to roadside vaginas on parade: to counter the dreariness, to resist death by boredom, to momentarily expel the bad breath from their many hours of solitude? What did years of roadside urine stops, to the music of chirping birds and speeding cars, the absent-minded inspection of his penis, shrivelled and sweaty, at times suddenly hard at the thought of what awaited in Alexandra, the trucker's dictatorial rod, randomly terrorising ant and termite holes, with coffee, Coca-Cola and watermelon water that had become urine, a salty puddle, discharged with vigour and relief, much to the terror of unsuspecting ants? It was perhaps the unbearable loneliness that pushed Father to once in a blue moon haul his flammable and explosive cargo through our neighbourhood, park the giant truck before our humble gate, and surprise Mother and I with a beaming smile and some carrot cake.

The presence of that truck worked wonders, because I suddenly became a sought-after friend to my playmates, fielding an avalanche of questions. Did the horse and trailer truly and really belong to my father? How come it had so many big wheels? What would happen if they placed their palms under the giant truck wheels when Father drove away? I joined them in exploring the truck. We, with our little palms, felt our way around the truck's massive wheel bolts (hot from the truck's coastal trek under the blazing sun), accidentally dipped our fingers in greasy nooks, cringed at the colour splashes, green and orange hues from murdered insects: decapitated dragon flies, upside down butterflies, disembowelled moths. Our little hands continued their caress of the massive machine, including the solid steel step onto which Father climbed into the tiny door, the twin exhausts that curved in front of the front wheels, shiny exhausts that hissed diesel smoke as Father wrestled the beast into submission.

We caressed, used lollipop sticks to dislodge tiny stones, glass bits and chewing gum lodged in the treads of the giant tyres. I was nagged. Persecuted with questions. Bribed. Allowed to get away with crimes – petty crimes. It was criminal the way I treated those playmates, how I took them for granted, instinctively knew they would seek me out, cajole me, betray each other, sell their tender souls, shower me with sweets, gang up and save me from clutches of bullies, put their ashy arms around my ungrateful neck. In whispers they pleaded . . . Could I speak to my father, ask him to on his next home stop please allow them petty (but in their view profound) privileges like to sound the truck's horn? Jiggle the steering wheel. Even a road trip, if at all possible.

I, as an unofficial Harmony Gas & Fuels representative, made sweeping and conclusive promises to my rascal friends; promises that, because of the mere existence of that truck, parked at our gate for an afternoon at most, guaranteed me novelties and loyalties reserved for very influential people. I lived like an emperor, surrounded by an ever-increasing galley of slaves, ring-wormed Mandelas and Churchills who worshipped my every gesture, no matter how laborious or erratic. Word of the truck spread to other streets, converting new disciples, eager entourages, whose only reward was a chance to caress the Harmony Gas & Fuels truck, to contribute to the urban legend of a truck that was like no other, a truck under whose carriage dusty rascals could lie, face up, counting bolts, sniffing at odd leaks, speculating why adults had hair in their armpits and, on daring occasions, confessions from Skinny Tefo, the discreet voyeur who wide-eyed and almost foaming at the mouth, yet in a whisper once said: 'They have hair down here, too! And my father likes wrestling mother on the bed, doing a funny dance on top of her. Mother closes her eyes, licks her lips, makes strange sounds, and says: "Yes, Daniel. My God in faraway heaven! Thank you for this man! Amen, you animal you. I am all yours. Harder! Just like that. Oh, you are good . . . In the beginning was the Word. Mercy, Mercy, Mercy! Through the gates of Jerusalem we shall walk. Mmm. Oh my precious Lord . . . Danny, Danny, oh God, I'm on fire!"'

'It's not funny sounds, stupid.' Our wisdom and enlightenment came from an unlikely source, the bow-legged Thomas, my scruffy disciple to whose bicycles I had unlimited access. 'They not wrestling, either. They're doing each other, making babies and things.'

'Really?' came a chorus from the unconverted.

'Yes, really,' confirmed Thomas. 'And . . .' he added, scratching his scaly limbs, 'they talk and breathe all funny. The men, too. I heard it's very nice.'

Pule stirred, shell-shocked: 'Like sweets?'

'No,' replied Thomas The Sage. 'Like many things mixed together. Sweets. Prayers. Juicy meat. Custard. Sugar cane. Flames. Like biscuits.

Sherbets. Wild animals. That's why they're always groaning, licking their lips. It must be that it tastes like many things at once.'

'You, Michael? You ever seen or heard anything strange? asked The Sage.

'No,' I answered curtly: 'My father is neither stupid nor a wild animal. Get away from under my father's truck, all of you!'

They shuffled away, the sorry creatures, dusting themselves, unsure when the truck would return, uncertain how long they had to keep up with me, their temperamental Emperor, under whose father's truck so many secrets lost potency. There was, after all the others were sent away, tails between their legs, but one disciple, Palesa, who remained behind, witness to the softer side of the Emperor, his sad eyes, the only one who would years later become her desk mate, witness epilepsy engulf her in heartless persecutions: clenched teeth and eyes that rolled back as of one possessed, the helplessness against those seizures she felt coming but could do nothing to stop, the river of urine that on some occasions wet her pristine uniform, travelled under shoes of disgusted classmates, as her body trembled to quake-like tremors.

The only thing that saved Palesa from total ruin, from being an object of pity and ridicule, was how strikingly beautiful she was – especially after her increasingly frequent seizures, when she looked exhausted, scared, dazed and confused, when I reached into my bag and, towel in hand, on all fours, followed the urine trail from puddle to stream to puddle, while teachers fanned her with notebooks. There were heartless attacks (snob, panty wetter, Ms Shakes!) against Palesa after school, from ugly cynics who envied her poise, her big tearful eyes, her beautiful mind.

'And you, Michael . . .' said Teacher Moleleki, 'are going to rule over these donkeys you have for classmates. Let them laugh, call you names, Urine Man or whatever, but you are going to rule over most people, and they will never understand why. What is even more beautiful, and I hope these frogs learn it sooner rather than later, is how consistent you have been as Palesa's friend. You have the purest of souls. Keep it up.'

Strong words. But the seizures kept coming, more frequent and violent, until I carried two towels, until the day Palesa almost chewed her tongue, that Teacher Moleleki spoke to her parents. She was taken out of school, never to return. It was later, when I was at the peak of my powers as Emperor under the Harmony Gas & Fuels truck, that she told me her secret passion: that she never intended to work for medical or audit firms, that she had no interest in solving cosmic puzzles or designing malls and whole cities, marketing toothpaste brands, but rather to spend all her days with animals, in oversized costumes and a red nose, a clown who was first and foremost a beloved friend of the circus animals.

I was, therefore, by the time I was at David Webster Hall, gravely offended by Rusty Bell's callous email, an email that insisted that I '. . . forget about this Palesa of yours and her circus charades', that further asked: 'Do you really want a clown for a wife, someone who befriends monkeys and camels for a living?' It was no accident that Palesa visited me, spent countless solidarity hours with me, while I lay fasting, starving. If there was anyone qualified to tell Dr West anything of substance, of value, it would have been Palesa. Yet I understood: Rusty Bell had, erroneously, over-estimated the power of her honey-brown assets and, unbeknown to her, committed a deplorable offence.

* * *

Frank had a car of his own once: an Idi Amin-type Mercedes, cream with red seats, bought with a Harmony Gas & Fuels loan, that ailed, blissfully rusted away on bricks under the mulberry tree, doubling as an extra laundry line and a urinal for Uncle Jonas, Father's drinker friend. The red seats were also a love couch for Palesa and I, when courting curiosities got the better of us. I – like Father and his Maria – in pleasant silence, held Palesa's hand from sunset to late night. There was residual heat at the back of the Amin Mercedes, embalming heat, heat that spurred my thoughts to cosmic heights, thoughts far removed from the dreary and often unpredictable pulse of the township. Mass funerals. Midnight arrests. Elaborate weddings. Police savagery.

One rainy night, I discovered the absolute bliss, the magnificence of nibbling pulsating ear lobes. Side by side, mouth to mouth, then mouth to ear, at the back of that Mercedes, built like a tank, its designer paraphernalia proclaiming: SE 500, Automatic. I would tell more of what transpired on that back seat, but a certain purity, a sacredness of sorts, does not allow me extended, elucidatory freedoms. Save for one insignificant, but nevertheless notable, detail: I learned that love has its own time zones, when six blissful hours may seem like minutes and, minutes (when love sours) like centuries. That drizzling evening was such a moment, blissful – except for the fact that Mr Mofokeng, Palesa's reputable motor mechanic father, was beside himself with anxiety. Fear. Anger even. Given Palesa's by-the-second death scares, it was to be expected that her father bordered on the paranoid – criss-crossing street after street, asking neighbours and passers-by, if they had seen a girl, in such-and-such a dress, or witnessed her convulsing, foaming at the mouth on some street corner.

Because extended explanatory liberties are relative, the petty but noteworthy detail continues as follows: when we did bump into her father, shortly after 11 p.m., on the corner of Sisulu and Ruth First avenues, sobbing silently as he walked, ghostlike because of the coal smoke that had descended over the houses, he couldn't help but hurl a screwdriver that almost punctured the cheek below my right eye. That is how I got the scar on my cheek, a scar shaped with the curvature of a euro symbol (€), without the two small lines, which distinctly separate my scar from the Euro zone currency.

There was a cold warning: 'Stay away from my daughter, or . . .' followed by trembling lips, a shaky warning finger, and a disjointed prayer: '. . . Palesa . . . Let's go home!' Prompt: calamities of the heart. My wiping urine off classroom floors, being mean to my disciples (for secretly making fun of Palesa's epilepsy), was never because I was in love. I did not wipe that steaming salty liquid, the colour of water, often times that of diluted apple juice because I in any way wanted to impress Palesa. I cannot say I was in love with her, but neither can I, with absolute certainty, say that I wasn't. Being with her left me with an odd feeling: not a singular feeling, but part warmth, part admiration, rock-hard trust, a familiar fondness – a pulsating submission to her charm that was pleasant yet overwhelming. It was not love, but something quite close, something easily mistaken for love, something much more grounded, a feeling that kept me awake for weeks on end, brooding, clutching at its elusive throbbings. Palesa was the closest thing to perfect feminine beauty. Come to think of it, she was the first woman for whom I bled. Touching.

* * *

Before my scar took shape, aping the euro currency, I had to make a futile trip to Sandton City to collect father's glasses, without which he was practically blind. Life was a blur, he said, shapes and colours deceptive, admiration of beautiful things curtailed. The optometrist, a Mr Jones, had sworn on his mother's grave that the spectacles would be ready three weeks following my screwdriver incident, but I was, upon arrival, advised by a visibly lazy or moody Victoria Taitz (such beautiful collarbones!) that Mr Jones had been arrested for medical-aid fraud, and that according to Eagle Vision's practice records, there were no glasses scheduled for collection by a Frank Somebody, or Frank Anybody.

Father complained that the frame on his spare glasses was heavy, aesthetically undesirable, and if truth be told, not consistent with the image he had of himself. When pressed for answers by his Maria exactly what that image of himself was, Frank laughed and, as was expected, said it was a long story, to be told some day in the future. 'That's my Frank,' interjected Mother. 'He believes he will live for two thousand years, answer everything in the future, talk day and night answering decades' worth of questions, some of which have long expired.' She gave him a mock frown, and said: 'But seriously, sweetie, why do you never answer questions?' 'Because,' chuckled Frank, 'what if words run out, from me answering every little thing? If I think about your questions, I can preserve words, like soldiers save ammunition. They, knowing enemy forces lurk around, don't waste bullets on frogs and lizards or target-shooting games on old rusty tins. So important is preservation of bullets that war tacticians invented bayonets, to stab and twist, puncture guts and fracture spines, a crude way of fulfilling one's war duties. It's the same with words; worse in fact: because there are no bayonets should they run out. A nod should be sufficient, most of the time, like would-be prisoners of war need only raise a white cloth, not recite the Book of Psalms, to be spared mortar rounds.'

These were not hollow speculations, for when not reading encyclopedias and aviation literature, Frank's other passion was reading about famous army generals. Westmoreland. Smuts. Rommel. Shaka Zulu. Yamamoto. MacArthur. He had, fleetingly, mentioned famous battles with deceptive interest: the firestorm of Dresden, the Battles of Moscow, Barbarossa and, with almost feverish delight, Operation Desert Storm. He must have observed I was puzzled by all the strange-sounding names, for he quickly mentioned, nodding to himself, that all he wished to share was that every battle has its tempo. Its horrors. Moments of beauty. A distinct smell. He paused, nodded some more, and said: 'Life is very much like that. Like war.'

This, unbeknown to him, once again propelled me to the Military History section at the Wartenweiler Library. I read about the fall of Berlin, the Red Army's rampage across Germany's ruins, the scale and terror of which got me thinking about Rusty Bell and her long fingers. It occurred to me that, as early as the 1940s, war-fatigued soldiers dished out not only bullets, but soiled German and wartime wombs with disdain, not because of any real need for sex, but because there were in abundance plump spinsters, widowed housewives and shell-shocked virgins whose only crime was being born with vaginas, into the depths of which the Russian infantry deposited the last tremors of Stalinism. Rusty Bell's crime was not committed in ruins, with my wrists pinned above my head, my protests silenced with gun-butting to the head until unconscious, until the last of fifteen-eighteen-maybe-twenty infantry men, pink buttocks squeezed tight to the magnetic pull of seeds defiling a body, then silence. And yet, Dr West's notes said nothing about such incidents, not even a lone footnote. How was he to be trusted, if he paid no attention to the minutest screams, even if these came from cupped mouths of Jovitas and Yettas, German mouths, ravaged as fleeting trophies of war?

It seemed Frank was not that dull after all, that there were some valuable secrets to his nodding, his Did-You-Know antics. 'Life is very much like war.' What does that mean? It was with these life-war speculations, Frank muttering some displeasure at having no glasses that fitted his image, that there was a knock at the door. The visitor looked burdened, remorseful. We sat around the now spacious wooden kitchen table, committed to samp and brown beans, our palettes assailed by the symphony of mother's beef stew. The visitor, whose conscience no doubt plagued him, declined a plate, requested a glass of water instead. As was normal in Alexandra, a tradition uprooted from the villages – Nongoma, Qunu, Ga-Mashashane and thousands of others – the visitor spoke about everything else other than what had brought him to our home: spiky bus fares, a toothache that had assailed him for the past three days, why did father let the noble Idi Mercedes rust and waste away, a cautious compliment to mother's age-defying figure, some reflections on the sinful price of red meat, before some absent-minded remarks on how by 'computerising everything' motor manufacturers were putting old-school mechanics out of work. That today's cars talk back, and know what ails them before the owner knows, warning that old-school practitioners in oily overalls were simply whiling away time with Ford Cortinas and Nissan Skylines with chronic carburettor ailments, for the hunger days ahead.

The ice-breaker conversations out of the way, Mr Mofokeng lowered his voice a decibel or two into grave mode, for discussion of matters both weighty and important. He told Frank and his Maria what they already knew, except that he had come to profusely apologise for nearly gouging my eye out, for acting so instinctively without foresight. He turned to me, said he had heard of the noble towel work I had been undertaking, that he was uninformed as to the true nature of my relationship with Palesa, that now that he knew he felt most ashamed for the euro currency predicament.

If I could find it in my heart, in my own time, which did not mean that he encouraged youthful and blind romance, he would be most humbled to be pardoned for the screwdriver mishap. What I and my family did not know, something he wished to inform us, was that he had been under extreme strain for years now, sleeping with one eye open, ears pricked, listening out for Palesa gasping in the dark. To my father he pleaded for pardon, to his Maria understanding, to me 'unreserved permission' to sleep better come night, knowing no one bore him any vengeance. My father turned to me, mentioned I was the wronged party, asked what my views were on Mr Mofokeng's apology, which sounded to me like practised grovelling.

'I forgive him,' I said without thinking. 'As long as he stays away from Palesa and me,' to which he, teeth clenched, perspiring, said he permitted that, within reason, but wished to retain a veto vote, to – like Truman – drop the Big One if he so wished.

That is how I always remember Mr Mofokeng: a grovelling mechanic facing extinction, masking cowardice by throwing screwdrivers at strangers. It was only after Frank had walked him out, that creature on the extinction list, his head hanging in shame, that father returned to share a few choice words – no doubt inspired by our visitor, the grovelling Ford Cortina expert who insisted on retaining veto votes: 'I have no one in mind in saying this, Michael, but I would much prefer, if it's within your nature, your sensibilities, that you pay particular attention to any man who walks around with unpolished shoes, laces undone, to say nothing of a beard left to run amok. It might not look like much, but the world has little sympathy for such characters. Love is blind, I know, but you will be surprised the number of headaches you will avoid, ten-fifteen years from now, by simply observing this seemingly insignificant detail. Just a thought.'

* * *

It was two years after leaving Harmony that Father studied past midnight, that Mother agreed it was worth risking all the family's lifetime savings (banknotes stuffed into an assortment of teapots), that Mother fixed those ties, kissed Father's forehead, her eyes searching his face for elusive charms, before her face eased into a loving, quavering smile. It was that routine, Father having walked away from the trucks, securing a wristwatch for fifteen years' service, that he almost flew aeroplanes, trained as air traffic controller at the then Jan Smuts Airport. It was because of his crack-of-dawn departures, his guiding pilots to land on which runways, to circle above Johannesburg in holding patterns, to delay take-offs, to anticipate hailstorms, that I finally stopped sleeping under tables, that father built a three-bedroom brick house, a house in which Columbus would be a tearful guest years later.

When Columbus visited, barely months before his passing, Frank sponsored an afternoon of good food and guarded conversations: that it was 'strange' that the Wentzels had no helper, Frank's friendly yet firm admonishing of misbehaving children that rained sand in Columbus' curls, the indiscreet questions Columbus asked: 'If you only had one room, one bed, where did Michael sleep?' Frank paused, composed himself, said, 'Under the table.' Then Father added reflectively, 'It's a tragedy of sorts, not bloody, but equally tragic.' It was the first time I ever saw Columbus bewildered, almost mute.

* * *

I knew no person, living or dead, as patient as my father. It was puzzling, heart-warming and at times infuriating how he – that Marvin Gaye lookalike – slowed time, crystallised it, to allow himself cerebral voyages, tranquil silences, too much time to listen to and *not* answer things. It was a peculiar patience, not without motion, not unlike that of aged fishermen brooding over fishing lines. In his siestas with time, slowing existence to endless shoe polishing and gardening passions (carrots, mushrooms), long evenings on the veranda on that squeaky rocking chair, his afternoon love affairs with Mother's roast beef, chunky portions of hours spent on leeches explaining that they had no money to pay him back year-old debts, Sunday mornings pouring over newspapers, followed by a game of cards and handholding with mother, the love of his life and envy of restless men. My father exuded the calm of a priest administering last rites.

* * *

I thought, brooded, reflected. Once my father qualified, nothing would give me greater pride than filling bureaucratic demands: Father's Name. Age. Occupation. It would have been magical, liberating, noble even, writing 'Trainee Air Traffic Controller', and not 'Truck Driver'. Bureaucrats silently sneered at truck drivers and, I suspected, dismissed my previous applications out of hand. What could a truck driver possibly offer the world? Not so with 'Air Traffic Controllers'! There would be curiosity, humility, misplaced familiarity in how questions will change from 'You do know such-and-such is not cheap . . .' to 'Excuse me, but what do air traffic controllers do?' I will always go for the most dangerous-sounding of answers, and watch as medical clerks and student accommodation administrators took note of the full implications of my enlightening them on the true value of air traffic controllers. There will always be a long pause, before I say: 'They prevent plane crashes.'

*　*　*

From: Michael@campus.ac.za
To: RustyBell@campus.ac.za
Subject: On Criminal Conduct

Rusty Bell,
There is no shred of doubt in my mind that you are a strikingly beautiful woman, and are yet to be even more so once you settle into a life of adulthood, which I suspect is an attempt at solidifying looks and character. A question has engulfed me in flames for years now, so much so that I cannot always tell when its tortures are of the mind or the soul. Or both. I am unsure what to call it, but Shakespeare has shed light on the insignificance of names: '. . . a rose by any other name . . .'

This question, or what I referred to in my previous email as Lifetime Quests, is in my view nothing complicated. I wouldn't, however, go so far as to say that its granular sparks, its essence, the very thing that makes it a fiery question, is not complicated. The question, which has in many ways deformed the person I suspect I was destined to be, has over time compelled me to think of myself in isolation from the universe. It might be worth your while to consider thinking of me not as you would a normal person with whom you almost pursued thunderous erotic ramblings. Think of me as a leaf, a healthy leaf glistening in the afternoon sun, brimming with pride, but at once defenceless against leaf-eating worms, against hailstones, windstorms.

That leaf, which hides the nakedness of trees, which with the change of seasons wilts away and dies, is sometimes all I perceive myself to be. I am yet to, if ever, make sense of what is to be expected from life, at once vibrant yet so unknowable. I think there is some beauty in that, in the elusiveness. Or is it just me, stewing in stupidity? I am in my fasts – or starvations, as you call them – capable of reaching the furthest frontiers of being, a journey so far into the depths of feeling I sometimes fear it will trigger madness. How majestic and addictive that feeling is, which – like space travel perhaps – seems so profound as to swallow me whole!

My journeys, the descent into unknown worlds, tunnels lit by streaks of purplish blue light, in total silence, is the most beautiful thing. It might very well be proven, in time, that our lives, the fleeting years we spend hypnotised by nipples and suffering, is but an insignificant footpath to delusion, for life is, or at least seems, elsewhere.

I am not, to my mind, beholden to life as you know it. The flame that has been seeking me, yanking me out of burrows of the mind, warming me with unexpected tenderness, charring me with relentless disdain, is the same question I wish to put to you – like a pin pricks skin, drawing blood, but not requiring that morticians be notified. The question is this: what is a leaf like me doing meddling in the affairs of the universe? If it is destined to wither and die, be trampled underfoot, unnoticed, shouldn't the leaf determine the extent and manner of its being, which is, as I have noted, too brief and vague? Why is it that my pursuit of new ways, to be a leaf on my terms, seems so futile?

Haven't you seen paintings of ancient Rome, of the Caesars, with their elaborate robes and gold ornaments, their stately heads crowned with leaves? Or leaves to accentuate flower gifts. Leaves on wreaths. A leaf to cover Adam's discovery of the treasures and terrors of nudity.

    Have you ever truly looked at a leaf, Rusty Bell, closely observed the minute pores that help it breathe? Have you run your fingers along its skin, let its tiny hairs, invisible to the human eye, caress your fingertips? Have you, on early mornings, noted dewdrops on leaves, droplets leisurely travelling down their veins onto the thirsty ground below? Have you, with undivided attention, observed your own eye reflected in bigger dewdrops, the size of infant palms? Have you ever noticed, during your morning waltz with nature, the slightest rustle from leaves rubbing against leaves in almost muted conversation? If you have, or at least thought about it, you will know that I am as delicate as a leaf, only much more fragile. In my burrowing, in pursuit of life elsewhere, of undiscovered beauty, there exists another world so tranquil, so fleeting, like invisible visions that momentarily make newborns wince, even smile in their sleep.

    So I am not capable of offering you what you want and perhaps deserve, because the path to such benefits is fraught with starvation. That said: why did you rape me? A savage, bleak, puzzling and hauntingly profane thing to inflict on another human being.
Conflicted,
Michael

* * *

Maria went to church every Sunday, returning late afternoon. It was the only time she stopped mending faulty zips, replacing missing buttons, fencing tyrannies on the garments of strangers. It was the only time she did not sketch pencil drawings, mind maps that would before our very eyes evolve into beautiful curtains intended for Melrose mansions, evening dresses for notable people, including a pretty young actress made famous by pretending to be a mother in a bath soap television advertisement. It was the only time that her sewing machine fell silent, that needles and colourful threads were stored away. It took time before she stopped accepting tailoring work, for the varied scents that accompanied strangers' clothes, odours that denied our house its distinct fragrance. The conflicting smells, on assorted garments, were eventually replaced by the inviting scents of rolls of new fabric: in creams, royal blues, in golds and shades of turquoise, their newness made prominent by patterns (leaf and flower impressions) yet to be burned and flattened by nanny irons.

On those Sundays, when Mother was at worship, Frank and I sat on the veranda, he on his rocking chair, encyclopedia in hand. He studied each entry with methodical familiarity, nodding, occasionally reaching for the teacup on a small table, on which lay World War II pictorials.

Then, one Sunday, he spoke out of the blue, as if addressing someone from the future. His tone hinted at sombre thoughts, moulded and sequenced, pressing in their immediacy, cautious while gently instructive. 'A Dr West telephoned me,' begun his address. 'Mentioned a lot of things, which I suppose are normal for a young man finding his feet in the world. Including the starvations – not an everyday occurrence, I admit, but not unthinkable. I was also telephoned by a Mr Bell, an uncouth and self-important man, impatient and inquisitorial, who alleges you are or were seeing his daughter, that you are refusing to take responsibility for a pregnancy. To Dr West I proposed closer examination of the facts; for I don't think you have become a madman overnight. He mentioned a salient point, which worries him greatly, that you believe a cat named Clinton something spoke to you? I imagine that is why he called me, in confidence, to fill in broad strokes, get a sense of your upbringing, the "home environment" as he put it.

'I'm not sure what to make of the cat incident, or the pregnancy, or the fact that you have been having difficulties, are under counselling, or why you chose to bear the burden alone, refrained from telling either me or your mother.' He paused, sipped his tea, said: 'I've known for some time, yet could not reconcile your calm persona with the apparent lunatic in waiting, as intimated by your psychiatrist. What I would like to say, should say, is that you can talk to me about anything, including speaking cats, whenever you are ready. Maybe cats speak, to particular people. I admit it is mind bending, but I suppose not unthinkable. Parrots speak, so why can't cats? By way of general comment, and I suppose unsolicited advice, the terrain of women can be ruthless business, or glorious existence, Michael. I suppose it's not too late to mention a few charms and pitfalls; perhaps out-of-date lessons on the vast courting empire.

'We were very lucky, my generation, in that the world had rigid expectations of women. Lucky is the wrong word. Perhaps it is better to say we benefited from the misery of our wives, sisters, mothers –

because our times enforced their unquestioning suffering. "You are a woman. Master the household. Open your legs. Shut your mouth." Maybe not that crude, but the sentiment holds. You wouldn't expect a traveller who has crossed a desert to, when water in presented, drink slowly, would you? So it's possible that your young lady, Busty or Musty, is not uncouth; that her lapses are the expression of your times, of women of your generation: a sudden gush, an unexpected explosion of water from neglected and rusting pipes, an outburst of freedom to do as one pleases – with unintended excesses.

'Most women, if not all, want to be loved – but for that love to be affirmed and recommitted over time, even when they don't, in certain moments, deserve it. Grounded companionship with your Busty, if you conclude she is the one, is not the hierarchy of opinions, yours over hers or vice versa, but the silences in between. Put plainly: grant her all her desires, without appearing to mould them to fit your sensibilities. Say she likes peach interior paint, you like berry red. Paint the house peach. You have no idea the lengths to which she would go to make you feel treasured. There are psychotic devils, of course, with whom you will never win, but generally speaking, women are not as impossible as they are made out to be.

'But I digress . . . There is no denying that some are capable of predatory acts, but that is generally a compliment, if a woman pursues you. She sees something in you, though she does not yet know it by name, its promise, its endurance. If there is one thing that you may consider learning, it is this: don't spend your life chasing lights. Dance in the shadows – you will soon see the deceptions of light.

'That is all I wanted to say. Think about it; use whatever has value, no matter how small. Lastly, don't tell Dr West or that Mr Bell person that I snitched on them. Things could get untidy. Its chilly out here, let's go back into the house.'

* * *

Finally, after 24 years of utter uselessness, Eugene found what seemed like a true gift, a talent of sorts. He quickly became the standard against which everyone else was measured, promoted, ridiculed. He was, to my knowledge, one of only a handful of people who travelled with the National Commissioner of Police to tense and daunting crime scenes, televised scenes requiring conciliatory and warning words from the highest authority. It was at such scenes, which demanded zero margin for error, that Eugene came alive, that he lay on his belly on adjacent buildings (behind chimneys, air-conditioning systems, solar panels); that he narrowed his eye into the scoped R1 rifle and, with a single shot, blew hostage-takers' heads to shreds. In banks. In homes. On city streets.

Those dirty green pupils of his were apparently able to see through anything – to anticipate the slightest movements, to – with a single squeeze of the trigger – ensure hostages live another day. But it didn't just happen. When Boni gave him grief and trashed the flat, Eugene blew off steam at The Cowboys, a shooting range off Louis Botha Avenue in Orange Grove. It was there that the owner, Big Ears Gouws, took notice, kept saying: 'Fuck! Been in this business for decades, and I never seen shit like this! D'you have lasers in those computer eyes of yours, Eugene?' Word got round. Bets were placed, money lost. How could this tall, bony, uninspiring creature pull off shots like that? How could he shoot tips off syringes suspended on twine, from such distances? He made money by ending lives, all the time shrugging off that his skill had become the stuff for sniper training manuals. Eugene was, when interviewed on those dreary crime-beat documentaries, equally uninspiring, his stock answer to the intricacies of his lauded marksmanship always a deflating, 'I just shoot the bad guy.' Peculiar that such trigger talent did not scare Boni; she spoke her mind, yelled at him if she felt she needed to, and loved her Eugene ever so tenderly.

* * *

Rusty Bell, who claims she lost her virginity to a tampon, derailed my life in ways I could have never imagined. There she came, in silk pyjamas, a mother, breasts surging with human milk, her face light years away from maternal happiness. That face mirrored a cocktail of feelings. Shock. Guilt. Fatigue. Uncertainty. Faint expectation. A turquoise scarf wrapped her dreadlocks, framing that round forehead of hers, those compliant eyebrows. I watched her eyes gather courage with every step she took, courage to, with a wifey, mature, strained smile, say: 'Hello, Michael.'

She joined us around the bed, where Catherine and Abednego sat side by side, not holding hands! How did they not do that, something that in some households came so naturally? Trapped in that maternity ward where Michael Junior was born three months premature, where I saw him battle to stay alive, I had a strange urge for violence. Michael Junior struggled on, oblivious to the soul exhaustion his father endured: fatigue of the very worst kind. Poor thing – besieged by drips to the fragile head, tubes and oxygen masks (feeding, ventilation), beeping machines monitoring blood pressure and heart rate, and the subdued lecture from Matron Khumalo, a lecture on the terrors of Respiratory Distress Syndrome, on neurosensory pitfalls that guaranteed a gloomy and expensive future, real and possible rails of cerebral palsy and attention deficit disorders.

'But,' she added, 'it's not a given. Most of the risks can be contained, even eliminated, thanks to advances in medical technology.'

I looked at Michael Junior. He looked like an electrocuted rat, head all veins with hints of tortured hair, scrawny body entangled in wires, in patches detecting and reporting things. He looked nothing like the babies back in the maternity wards, the readily lovable ones who didn't break your heart, brimming with newness and innocent scents.

'Why?' asked Abednego.

The lecture continued: 'Premature rupture of membranes, foetal abnormalities are also contributing factors – though some cases are triggered by lifestyle and environmental risks.'

My heart sank. Poor thing: hanging onto life by the fingernails.

* * *

Incidents at Milpark Hospital landed me back on Dr West's couch. I had been eating, I told him, slowly at first, until the body started recovering, blossoming. I had not fasted for 90 days straight – and looked forward to the home-cooked meals Palesa brought. She was seeing a young music executive at the time, Quentin, a well-mannered gentleman with an infectious laugh.

Three days a week Quentin's Volvo stopped off at the Johannesburg Zoo and picked up Palesa and her succulent dishes, a Palesa who was growing to be quite an obvious catch, whose epilepsy had decided she had suffered enough. My protests that she not continue bringing food was met with firm resistance, and Quentin, in his religious ways, insisted that service of others pleased the Lord. So they fed me, Palesa and her Quentin, to a point that I completely stopped going to the dining hall, and became oblivious to the Cheese Committee and their charades.

As I lay on Dr West's couch, counting ceiling partitioning, my palms resting on my belly, I suddenly had questions. I let him speak at length about his understanding of the issues at hand, assure me that the Michael Junior issue was not of my making, talk about giving oneself permission to accept the world as it is. Audrey brought mint tea, which only sharpened questions that had been tormenting me for days. They weren't questions in the strictest sense, but thoughts that like a shoal of fish sped past my mind, each thought its own, but also part of the black mass that twisted and turned at alarming pace: why did I have a sudden predisposition to violence? What did he understand by the concept of a pure soul? Was a soul, clear as light, one with moral authority? Wouldn't he, I asked him, agree that Rusty Bell's *coup d'état* constituted a moral Problem, that that being so, my troubles were existential rather than psychological? He sweated. Winced. Fidgeted.

'A pure soul? I don't know, Michael. You would have to speak to a priest about that. I wouldn't, in all honesty, know where to start. Moral, existential and psychological crisis? Those are very difficult questions. I suppose you're right, if you feel resolute and strong enough about what you say. I cannot be quick to affirm or deny. That is not how I work. My wish is to give you tools to help you cope with these setbacks, without harm to you and those around you. I believe we've made tremendous progress. As for violence, the urge to be violent is often times an expression of frustration, though the triggers are numerous and varied. That can partly be overcome by channelling those negative and destructive thoughts into positive and pleasant experiences. Something as simple as enjoying a meal. Look at you – you're a picture of good health.'

I thought about his answer, and then countered: 'Camus says there is but one truly philosophical question and that is suicide.'

'He says that?'

'Yes. Judging whether life is or is not worth living amounts to answering the fundamental question of philosophy.' That couch was comfortable, massaging me to further ask: 'What d'you think about that, Doc?'

He fidgeted a little more and, taking notes, said: 'I suspect that that's not all branches of philosophy. I am not a great fan of Albert, Michael, so my answer would be biased. It is a loaded statement no doubt, but I'm not sure I share the same sensibilities. What does it mean to you?' I said I would think about it, after which that brilliant bastard hinted that our time was up, confirmed by Audrey, who stated that a Mr Rabinowitz was already waiting. I shook his hand and left.

Rabinowitz? What could possibly be bothering him: what depravities, which raging appetites, what persecutions?

* * *

I was traumatised by the hospital visits, yet still felt guilty if I didn't go to see Michael Junior, that creature with its fast breathing, those defective lungs overworking, the little stomach rising and falling at alarming speeds. Matron Khumalo said he was doing very well, growing faster than expected, said he was a little fighter. It was hard to understand what she was talking about, for in my eyes the poor thing was suffering. No amount of assurance changed the fact that I knew suffering when I saw it. Doing very well? What could that possibly mean, for even in grades of distress, for which there are no reliable measurements, the least serious remained solemn, surely?

Matron Khumalo was perhaps comparing Michael Junior to similar or worse cases she had seen, which was for me, a problem. This particular suffering, of this evidently handsome mouse, a snoozing work of art, at once repulsive but increasingly adorable, was his and his alone. Mathematics could not apply to suffering; it simply was not divisible, comparable. 'He is doing supremely well,' reiterated the matron, as if reading my thoughts. I was aware, as I contemplated the matron's assurances, that some if not most of Camus' thoughts would be outdated, irrelevant, that quoting them from memory meant nothing and that, as with all well-meaning people before and after him, such thoughts remained precious but out of touch, their subdued potency a mockery of philosophy itself. Life, ideas – as that brilliant bastard pointed out – had a lot to do with sensibilities: accords and denials of a personal and secretive nature.

There was, in my excavations of the mind, another distressing discovery: that my life's arc had, until then, resembled that of my father. Was Frank's advice sound simply because he had walked the same path, or was it genius from another source? I wished he could be forthright in his counsel, firmer, more conclusive. What were those open-ended positions of theirs, his and Dr West's?

Comparatively, you couldn't fault Rusty Bell in her positions: 'I have no more lectures for the rest of the day; you can have me if you want.' Failing which I would just rape you. And then be both delighted and genuinely remorseful. But Rusty Bell had new concerns, obscure 'wife' apprehensions, warnings of which were expressed with devastating clarity: 'I know you're very intelligent, Michael. But that's not always a good thing. You're going to think yourself to death.'

* * *

The matron had been right. That electrocuted creature was blossoming to good health before our very eyes. Then one day Rusty, ever so slightly, reached for my hand; held it in a not-so-tight, not-so-limp clasp, leaned her head on my shoulder, smelt me in a silent, non-intrusive way. She raised her eyes from the comfort of my shoulder, released my hand, embraced my waist, and rubbed the ribs, the space between armpit and waistline. She smiled, and those dimples sank in their programmed sequence, their distinct duties of making her absolutely stunning: the one to the right of her lower lip, then the one left of her chin and, finally, the two wells that momentarily dissolved the centre of her cheeks. Something shifted inside of me, something important. It seemed a permanent shift, a movement both sudden and profound. Was it forgiveness, love maybe? It could have been defeat, surrender, but one never knows with these things. I could not rule out loneliness, suspected fatigue, and yet knew, instinctively, that the answer would take time, become apparent, on its own terms.

* * *

My 44th consultation was not without beauty. Audrey seemed sad, nervous, in shock as she ushered me into Dr West's room, where he sat waiting. His right arm was in a plaster, his fingers trapped and swollen in a cast. A bruise smudged his right temple, his lower lip swollen. He stood, limped past his desk, taking a pen and notebook from his table. He seemed rattled yet jovial, at times distracted and introspective. There was a cut (four stitches) on his shin, one he gently scratched as he sat down for the session. He, to manage curiosities I suppose, mentioned in passing that he had received a sound beating from one Mr Rabinowitz, the trigger unknown. 'Rabinowitz with the rabbi beard and one short leg? Walks with a stick, fidgety, grass-green suit. That Rabinowitz – here this past Wednesday?' I asked.

Dr West smiled, a crooked swollen-mouthed grin: 'Yes, him. That stick of his proved particularly handy, in almost fracturing bones. He believes I've ruined his life, at least that is what he kept saying as he rained blows on me. But you must understand the man's unwell, mentally questionable. Risky business, psychiatry. You never know.' Witty, that Dr West, the understated charm expressed in a controlled, circumstantial lisp. 'Yes, Michael, I guess there is a time to help, one to be beaten up for helping. My ribs. That Mr Rabinowitz sure knows how to kick.'

'Will you continue seeing him?'

'Oh, yes. Rather me than innocent bystanders. He'll come around. Most eventually do.'

I was stunned. And, as a way of easing into a taboo subject that hovered over my consultations, that of my rape, asked him if there was a difference between moral Problems and Questions. He smiled, said he did not know, but supposed moral Problems were more immediate – that is, both Problem and Question in one. He believed Questions implied that there was some time to reflect, debate. Protestors filled streets chanting for rights to abort unwanted babies. That, he said, were moral Questions. It could not be compared with Jews, Rabinowitz's ancestors, being gassed to death in their millions. That, he said, was a moral Problem that needed immediate correction. He asked me, when I had shared my readings on Red Army atrocities, if I thought Rusty Bell was a rapist. I couldn't say for certain, I told him, but supposed true rapists would not rest their head on your shoulder, smell you, readily admit to their crimes. Strangely, madly perhaps, I had in an odd kind of way reasoned that my episode, the Rusty Bell coup, was perhaps karma gone wrong, that I was perhaps, wrongly, being held accountable for the 1940s' plunder of Yettas and Wilmas by the Red Army. Those screams, those ready tears against defilement, the midnight sobs under beds, in crammed and dusty attics, against an advancing plague: dresses ripped with army knives, breasts licked and faces spat upon, in payment for The Führer's sins. He, Adolph, did not seem to be bothered, smiling meekly in those grainy black-and-white documentaries, pinched cheeks of child soldiers last in line to defend Germany, against men with red flags and itchy groins. It must have been payment for muted screams of Uwimanas and Mukantagaras, Rwandans, ravaged in refugee camps, hacked and defiled, a fee I was paying for an ancient crime dating as far back as biblical times. Did it matter, numerically and statistically, if one Rusty Bell had her way with me?

'Yes,' said Dr West, emphatically. 'Two wrongs do not make a right. But there is such a thing as burying the hatchet. I'm sure Stalin was embalmed never having heard of you. You were not even born. How could you possibly pay for old sins not remotely linked to you in any way, shape or form?'

'But isn't the world connected across time and place?'

'Michael . . .' he said, a touch impatient, 'should I now blame the Pope for Rabinowitz's enthusiasms?'

We both laughed. He winced with pain, said he believed Rusty Bell was good natured and kind, that though not explicitly saying he recommended matrimony, he believed it was worth careful examination, worth considering. He was also quick to remind me that it was now a three-way decision, that fatherhood also implied that, by his mere presence, Michael Junior could force my hand in ways I never thought possible. This turned out to be a roundabout way of him asking if I loved the child, to which I, with brutal honesty, said: 'I have my moments.'

'Meaning what exactly? Does it perhaps mean you're warming up to Rusty?'

'You're asking me to define, to draw a line between multiple, conflicting feelings. How is that possible?'

'No. I am asking you if you love the child?'

'Love has its burdens. So, in so far as children are innocent creatures, yes.'

'Let's try a yes or no answer, please.'

I felt cornered, thirsty, and said: 'No.'

Dr West took off his spectacles, rubbed his eyes. He felt his swollen mouth with the back of his hand and, strained but composed, reiterated: 'That Rabinowitz fellow sure knows how to express his displeasure.' He adjusted his broken arm, cradled in a sling and, almost inaudible, said: 'I hear you. But keep in mind you're only 24 years old, Michael. Shouldn't such finality be reserved for 70-year-olds, with little or nothing to lose?'

But he was wrong, yet again. Seventy-year-olds have a lot to lose: memory, libidos, other 70-year-olds. It was only, with the session ending, that I saw two men in suits and dark shades sitting hawk-eyed in Dr West's waiting room: bodyguards. Against that unpredictable Rabinowitz. Maybe. I had only one thing in mind: sleep.

* * *

I lay in bed thinking. Grill Restaurant Lucy. Airport Prune-Boobed Isabella. Midnight Dulcinea. Did these names, distinctly separated by place, time of day and body parts, point to Dr West's other, discreet life? Or were they innocent friends? It was, to me at least, unthinkable that Dr West was a typical man, defenceless against female charms. Or did Isabella assign herself more functions, other than checking the Doctor's flight tickets and luggage? Did she look him in the eye, coy and suggestive, her chest positioned for prominence, a sustained smile on her face and, say, 'Enjoy Barbados, Dr West. Come say hello sometime. It can get very lonely around here.' Would such vague, open-ended words have been enough to ensnare or arouse him? Would he have, unlike me, paid attention to Isabella's discreet invitation: Enjoy. Come. Say. Hello. Very lonely. It will never be known what he or she said, but it was a confirmed fact that she was employed at or passing through the airport, with breasts that made the Doctor think of prunes, thus transforming her into a muse. And yet the same man, skilled in milking airport encounters, nudged me to accept arrangements, a lifetime with Rusty Bell, for which I had neither passion nor control. 'There is such a thing as burying the hatchet,' he had said. What hatchet? Why was I supposed to be burying hatchets I had nothing to do with? I would have none of it!

* * *

Love has its burdens and, in so far as children are innocent creatures, yes – I had my moments. I knew what was coming for me: the dreadful names, the judgements, the cutting stares. The prelude was already in Dr West's eyes, his discreet search for parental affirmations: do you love the child? Why was there – as if my burdens weren't back-breaking already — an expectation, of preordained love demands, a yoke that would grind my neck with each step I took?

I, futile as this was, wished to state — without contradiction and with a clear conscience — that I had very conflicted feelings as far as Michael Junior was concerned. As hard as I tried, fasts and meditations included, I could not accept that I had the slightest inclination to be, or the remotest idea of how to be, a father. Dr West had completely misunderstood my Question-versus-Problem prognosis on issues of morality. This was the sole reason I had refrained from asking him about the third dimension, that of moral Dilemmas, which were neither Questions nor Problems. For every cave I squeezed into — shielding myself from Abednego's bloodshot eyes following me everywhere, Rusty Bell's relentless nagging, her nudges — there seemed to be a conspiratorial light that searched my darkest corners. That light, harsh and dizzying, was what I tried running from in refusing Rusty Bell's intimacies, intimacies that were by their nature unknowable. Her insistence and life's complicity, its entrapments in soul-denting affairs, in matrimonial snares, in-law cages, in mortality yokes, in fatherhood dungeons, under lust guillotines, in cerebral furnaces that produced no ash (where was the evidence of burning?), in freedom tombs, was what I had dreaded ever since I followed Palesa's urine trail as it meandered its steamy voyage on dusty classroom floors, under raised shoes and across cement cracks, taking lone grass ears and sand granules with it. Why couldn't Rusty learn from Palesa's example? Palesa, who even when exceedingly grateful at my urine duties, had no expectations beyond our mutual 'understanding' — an understanding Teacher Moleleki overstated as something to do with pure souls. I never had a conclusive opinion on this, except a minor jolt of vanity that jabbed the spine, at almost being sanctified.

I cannot say that I was completely immune to Rusty's advances, her cravings. Part of the torment, which Dr West seemed determined to explain away, was the fact that I was unwilling to violate dictates of my conscience, to not – even when facing complete obliteration – stand by my resolve and the purest of truths: that I had been ambushed into pleasures and their aftermath. My whole being was, at the time, far removed from anything resembling the drudgery of paternity – not because of any loathing I have for infants but because I wanted the conception of such beings to never be such an erratic, tyrannical affair. At the age of 24, I refused to be, over and above blatant violations, further enslaved – be mined for a love I neither possessed nor understood.

It was after considerable wrangling between Rusty Bell and I, Frank and Abednego (emissaries, meetings, tempers, death threats, compromises) that it was agreed that Michael Junior would, upon release from hospital, be raised as my little brother by Frank and his Maria. That it was obvious that I refused any entanglements and would, if pushed, seek justice for my rape, which had until then been my undisclosed anguish. There was blackmail, accusations of being stone-hearted, but the facts dictated that there was more than met the eye. That all the huffing and puffing could not dissuade all involved that the matter at hand was not limited to Rusty's carnal espionage, but that if properly dissected pointed to profound philosophical postulations complex enough to occupy us over three generations.

Were there definitive grounds to conclude rape had indeed occurred? If so, were there moral obligations on me to participate in my own enslavement, my execution? Were there impartial arbiters to weigh the facts, to decide, with an eye on implications 20, 30 years into the future? In practical terms, what did it mean that Michael Junior would be raised as my brother? If Michael Junior was to be raised as my brother, what – as Abednego rightfully asked – was the distinction between make-believe brotherhood and the reality of my predicament? Couldn't the whole dispute, if it was that, be amicably resolved using common sense and logic? Which took precedence between the two: common sense or logic?

Throughout the wrangling, my thoughts often drifted away from discussions at hand, as I followed a neighbour propelled by the toils of laundry, rinsing and re-rinsing before, humming Joan Armatrading ballads, she began hanging garments on the line: two red blouses in quick succession, baggy brown breeches, a purple blouse, cream tracksuits, a long sequence of floral pyjamas and disfigured T-shirts and, between the clothes, covertly, a generous instalment of lacy lady knickers in variations of earthy tones and yellows. These were promptly followed by two brassieres, one white, the other a pinkish-purple. Pinkish-purple. A safe, in-between colour, not grandmotherly, but at the same time not as passion inflicted as reds and silverfish-golds. I knew those hands, securing socks and pillowcases to the washing line, those industrious hands rinsing pyjamas in buckets, the same hands that clutched my wrist, pulled me into that darkish room, heavy with smells of floor polish, those alert eyes that stared me down in fondness and purpose, that mouth that implored me to keep a secret, that told me I was unlike other kids, that I was chosen, special. I was, at fourteen, confronted by the spectacle and mystery of a naked woman, full grown and tipsy. It was true. They have hair down there. It was this confirmation, what followed, that completely derailed my life. There was, long before Rusty Bell, an unassuming neighbour: the discreet, patient, lonely Auntie Pauline, through whose covert operations all subsequent nude women seemed to smell of floor polish, a sour belch of beer. I had to be jolted back to the meeting by my father who, sipping tea, gently said: 'You still with us, Michael?

SIR MARVIN AT 50

The thing with Auntie Pauline is this: there are reasonable grounds to suspect that she might, in fact, have been a loving and generous person. But on that specific afternoon, Auntie Pauline, to whom I am not related by blood, drunk and determined, soiled her unconfirmed reputation, a reputation that might in hindsight not stand scrutiny. I have long discounted the beer as a motive, for truly drunk people are not that eloquent, that persuasive; neither are they so assured and steady in gripping the wrists of would-be sacrificial lambs. That room that smelled of floor polish. That gut, those horrid, giant concertina folds that lined her body, the knickers she skilfully folded into a ball, slid under the pillow. Those searching, pleading eyes of hers, their determination, her minute pauses, her conflicted conscience, that quivering, motherly, unlikely-lover voice, that repulsive beer belch, is a nightmare I still wake to these days.

I visit my parents once in a while. Pensioners now, they are ageing gracefully, still hold hands, still play cards. My father never did make it as an air traffic controller. He was, when final selection time came, overlooked on the basis of age and bad eyesight, something that has left him fragile. Blessed with good health, Frank and his Maria are the cheapest souls to maintain. They have an unexplained aversion to luxuries, an obsession with that handholding of theirs. Auntie Pauline still lives alone. Petrus, her husband, will not be released on medical parole. She does not remember him, being senile and all. Maria says it's very sad, Frank simply nods. Someone has to move Auntie Pauline from the sun, Mother says, for she has a bad leg.

It might as well be me. Auntie Pauline hears the gate clutter, footsteps as I approach.

'Who's there?' she asks startled.

'A friend. I've come to move you to the shade, off the lawn,' I say. She is thin as a rake. Maybe it's the tuberculosis. I lift her to her veranda, and seat her on a plastic chair. She does not recognise me. She has aged, has a violent cough, her foot trembles. She signals for a water jug; drinks in between intermittent coughing. She takes my hand, squeezes it, and says: 'God bless you, Friend.' She cocks her head, asks: 'Is Friend your name?' A cat walks by, tiptoeing, cautious.

'No, that's not my name.'

'What's your name?'

'Sir Marvin.'

She doesn't seem to have heard, mutters something incoherent.

*　*　*

Every war has its own pace, its own smell. What does that mean? I cannot say I'm completely cured. There are evenings when I cannot help yearning for Desirable Horses, to see Simone. Thompson

Buthelezi & Brook telephone me every week. I tell them and other law firms the same thing: that I don't want to be a lawyer any more. Rusty is doing important diplomatic work with Michael Junior. He is a lot calmer these days, and says: 'Please come listen to this piece of music, Dad. Tell me what you think?' or 'Thank you for the grand piano, Sir Marvin, it's really beautiful.' My Arabic is really good now. Rusty salutes me for refusing to read important things in translation. I could have been addicted to porn, a translation of the goings on at Desirable Horses. But it was much better being there. It is possible that Auntie Pauline's wrist grabbing will be a thing of the past, no more than a bad memory.

I thank God for that open window. Who knows what would have happened? Many would have survived, brushed the incident aside, dismissed it as a drunk woman out of her depth. Not me. It's true, you know – I'm extremely sensitive, particular about everything. Always have been.

* * *

Michael Junior and I are interviewing piano teachers tomorrow. I want him to be a proper composer. I do not need a gun or whisky bottle for that. The piano will play well if the right keys are known and mastered. Such beauty, piano music, is not dependent on Simone and her banknote frowns. Simone, Simone: those collarbones – my God. But are they better than Rusty's? Well, maybe a little, in very small, negligible ways. Or maybe it is too dangerous to compare collarbones? That brilliant bastard might know.